A Second Chance Scottish Summer

A Short Novel

Rachel Mae Linden

"An enchanting tale about the one thing we've all imagined: a magical second chance. Rachel Linden expertly mixes romance, mystery and family-drama into a delicious recipe of a story. With her trademark warmth, Linden delivers a captivating story with a magical heartbeat at its center."

—Patti Callahan, *New York Times* bestselling author of *Surviving Savannah*

"Magic, sweet treats, heartfelt charm . . . this dreamy tale has it all!"

—*Woman's World*

"*Recipe for a Charmed Life* is actually a recipe for a magically marvelous read about expectations, second chances, and following your heart. Rachel Linden writes complicated and compelling characters that are as relatable as they are likeable. I enjoyed every bit of this delightful novel."

—Jenn McKinlay, *New York Times* bestselling author of *Summer Reading*

"The perfect mix of delicious backdrop details, family secrets, and the quest for purpose and lasting love. Enchantingly delightful from first page to last."

—Susan Meissner, *USA Today* bestselling author of *Only the Beautiful*

"Rachel Linden whips up an irresistible family drama oozing with charm and magic! *The Magic of Lemon Drop Pie* is a must read for anyone who longs for second chances. A gem of a novel that charmed me from [the] get-go, perfect for fans of Sarah Addison Allen and Alice Hoffman."

—Lori Nelson Spielman, *New York Times* bestselling author of
The Star-Crossed Sisters of Tuscany

"A delicious read, down to the very last lemon drop! Rachel Linden delivers a delightful escape, wonderful characters, and a magical experience that will leave readers hungry for her next book."

—Julie Cantrell, *New York Times* and *USA Today* bestselling
author of *Perennials*

"Completely charming! Take a spunky heroine, add a swoonworthy, orange-rubber-overall-wearing oyster farmer, throw in a dash of the real-life messiness we all understand, and sprinkle a dusting of Linden's signature magical realism, and you've got the recipe for a delightful story you can't put down."

—Katherine Reay, bestselling author of *A Shadow in Moscow*

"A deliciously sweet tale about refusing to give up on your dreams and finding your bliss against all odds. Linden gives readers so much to enjoy—romance, family drama, and bitter-sweet second chances—all served up with the perfect dash of magic."

—Kate Bromley, author of *Here For the Drama* and
Talk Bookish to Me

Other novels by Rachel Linden

A Second Chance Scottish Summer

Rachel Mae Linden

1 st paperback and e-book edition April 2025

Book Cover design by Kristin Bryant

ISBN 979-8-9985734-1-5 (paperback)

ISBN 979-8-9985734-0-8 (ebook)

Published by Rachel Linden

www.rachellinden.com

*For all the readers who raised their hands when I asked,
"Who wants to read a love story about a hunky ginger Scot in a
kilt making cheese?"*

This one's for you.

Chapter 1

"Ciao," I murmur regretfully, watching another broken dream walk out the front door of the now almost-empty gelato shop. This time it's a fancy gleaming silver gelato maker the moving crew is lugging out to the waiting truck. New, the machine retails for over seven thousand dollars. I've managed to sell it secondhand for two-thirds the retail cost. Hailey, the owner of the charming but sadly unprofitable Golden Gate Gelateria, is very grateful to get at least a good portion of her investment back. The sign on the front door of the shop says "Closed." This time it's permanent.

I dip my tiny plastic gelato shovel into a scoop of very tart, very delicious lemon gelato and take another bite. It's a shame the business couldn't turn a profit. The gelato is very tasty. We're eating the last of the inventory while we oversee the movers. Soon this shop will be just another empty storefront. I sigh. Sometimes my job feels so depressing.

"I think that's it, boss lady," Enrique, the chief mover, tells me, stopping inside the front door and wiping his brow. It's raining outside, and he's soaked. "Just the tables and chairs left. Then we're done."

I glance around the little shop. It's an adorable room painted in mint, mango, and cream, with whimsical striped wallpaper and a throwback vintage vibe. It's sad to see such a cute place get stripped of everything of value. Beside me, Hailey is sniffling gently as she works her way through the last scoop of wild strawberry gelato.

"Avery, thank you," she says softly. Her eyes are red rimmed and puffy. She's been crying watching the movers clear out the storefront. "I don't know what I would have done without you."

I brush off the compliment. "I'm sorry you're having to close up shop," I tell her sympathetically. I really am. Just because I'm good at dismantling people's dreams and squeezing as much cash as possible from failing food-based businesses doesn't mean I like it.

In the ten years I've been doing this job, I've liquidated everything from Michelin starred restaurants to mom-and-pop donut shops. These final days are always the most painful for owners, seeing all they've worked so hard for get dismantled piece by piece. I know firsthand the bitter taste of failure, the heartbreak of all those dollars and hours amounting to nothing in the end.

In my mind's eye I see a familiar royal blue storefront facing the curve of Oban Bay. *The Thistle Tearoom: family-owned since 1905* is etched on a sign over the door. A **For Sale** sign is taped slightly askew on the big plate glass window. The image, even a decade later, brings with it a quick, fresh stab of shame and sorrow that takes my breath away.

I force my attention back to the present, reminding myself of why I do this job. I can't save a doomed business venture, but I can soften the blow with a little cash cushion and a helping hand. Tonight, this storefront will be vacant, and Hailey will be left with an aching disappointment and some big existential questions about her next steps in life. But thanks to me, she's not drowning in unpaid debt or facing bankruptcy. I negotiated her out of the storefront lease with only a small penalty, and after selling off all the equipment and paying my consultation fee, she'll be able to walk away with minimal financial loss. It's the best she could hope for in this situation. It's what I wish someone would have done for me all those years ago. Unfortunately there was no one to bail me out then. I had to figure it out, heartbroken and alone. I don't want anyone to feel like that.

My phone rings, and I glance at the screen. It's the office. I've worked for the same business liquidation consultancy for the past decade since coming back to the States from Scotland. Most likely it's Betty, the office administrator, calling with my next assignment. This current closure is a fairly small job. I've been in San Francisco just a few days handling the gelateria. Tomorrow morning early I'll head back to my apartment in Chicago for the weekend, then fly out Sunday night or Monday for a new location. The sad truth is that there's always something closing somewhere in the country, so my services are constantly in demand. I hope it's somewhere warm this time. April in San Francisco has been chilly and wet. The weather here reminds me of Oban, actually. Maybe I'll get lucky and this next job will be somewhere warm and southern.

Just wrapping this up. Send details re next assignment. Hoping for sunshine. I text Betty. I include a string of smiling sun emojis.

She texts back **How about a chain of three failing sports bars in Milwaukee? Owner had a heart attack. Heirs want to liquidate.**

I grimace. Sounds straightforward and boring... and probably cold. However, Milwaukee is only an hour and a half drive from my condo in Chicago, so I wouldn't even need to fly.

Stifling a sigh, I text her back. **I'll drive up on Monday.** Then I tuck my phone away and turn back to Hailey. She's watching mournfully as Enrique and his guys hustle the tables and chairs into the waiting van. I've found a buyer who is renovating a macaron shop and agreed to purchase all the furniture.

"How do I start over?" Hailey asks me quietly. "I've spent the last five years working to make this shop a success. I don't have any idea what to do now."

I recognize the lost look in her eye. I remember feeling that way before I found my feet again, before I figured out how to turn my failure into a different kind of success. One that doesn't bring that bright, happy fizz of joy and satisfaction, but at least it pays the bills and helps other people in their hour of need.

"You find something else you're good at," I tell her gently but firmly. "And you learn to live with the failure. Trust me, you'll find something new. Maybe it won't be your dream, but sometimes we don't get our dream. Sometimes we make do and get the next best thing."

I don't tell her I know this from hard-won experience. I don't tell her that often the regret still gnaws at me, alone in another hotel room or short-stay apartment. I could not save our beloved family business after Aunt Ellen's sudden passing. She left me her treasured tea shop and I drove it into the ground within a year. I'd give anything to know what I know now, to have a chance to redeem myself, to turn back time and redo my mistakes. But it's too late. I mucked it all up years ago. Now I have to live with the consequences every day.

"I hope you're right," Hailey says doubtfully.

"I am," I tell her with a calm confidence born from experience. I don't confess my secret though. I can't even acknowledge it to myself, the truth that there is some small part of me, a tiny stubborn part that still hopes for something more than this. Somewhere deep inside, I still crave the joy of helping a dream grow and thrive instead of just being a scavenger, stripping the carcass of a shattered vision once it's dead. But hope is dangerous. Hope is risky. I can't handle failure again. The last time shattered my life and I left Scotland for good.

Since then, I've been careful never to risk that much again. I'm determined to stick to what I'm good at, even if my chest aches some days with the longing for more. With a sigh I tuck that dangerous little hope away in the farthest corner of my heart, scrape the last of the tart lemon gelato from the bowl, and get back to work dismantling another failed dream.

Chapter 2

Blocking the harsh, keening Highland wind off the moors with his tall, muscled body, Laird Lachlan pressed Gemma back against the cold stones of the castle keep, his brooding eyes darkening with desire. She could feel him through the heavy tartan wool of his kilt, hard muscle and sinew against her petticoats. He wanted her. That was abundantly clear.

She couldn't seem to catch her breath... Lachlan MacGregor, the laird of the manor and her clan's sworn enemy, was pressing so close she could feel the heat of him against her delicate flesh. Her senses were filled with the scent of him – leather and shaving soap and heather. He leaned closer still, his breath warm against the soft skin of her throat.

"I'll have you yet, lass," Lachlan whispered, and Gemma shivered as she felt the words sink into her heart, a threat or a promise...

The jingle of my phone snaps me back to reality with the peppy blaring notes of The Spice Girls *Spice Up Your Life*. I drop the historical romance novel I'm reading like it's a hot pan and scramble for the phone on my nightstand, knowing exactly who is calling me. My sister Poppy programmed this music into my phone the last time I visited her in Oban five years ago. I never changed it. *The Laird's Revenge* flutters to the bed, cover face up, showing the hero and heroine locked in a passionate, half-clad embrace amongst the windblown heather. I flip the book over to conceal the creamy swell of her bosom and the rippling muscles of his bare torso above his kilt.

"Hey Pops,"

My sister's pretty, freckled face fills the phone screen. "Hey big sis!" she says cheerfully, as if it's been days and not months since we last spoke. "Ooh, I like your hair. You know that ash blonde tone is so popular these days. Lucky you!" She cocks her head. "And I like the curtain bangs. They suit you."

"Thank you," I preen a little. The dishwater blonde natural color of my hair has, thanks to Taylor Swift, been dubbed "old money blonde" and suddenly become super popular.

"What are you up to this weekend?" Poppy asks. She's sitting outside on the front stoop of Haye House, our ancestral family home on the west coast of the Scottish Highlands. I recognize the warm golden stones of the grand entrance behind her. The house was built in the mid 1850s and has been in our family ever since. A sprawling, slightly shabby Scottish baronial manor perched on a hill above the charming coastal town of Oban, it boasts commanding views of the village and the sea. It's where our dad and his older sister, our Aunt Ellen, grew up just like generations of Hayes before them. Now Poppy and her husband and twins live there.

"Um... I'm at my apartment." I kick the romance novel off the bed and it lands on the rug next to the unzipped suitcase where I keep my ever-growing secret collection of romance novels stashed away under my bed. Not a soul in this world knows how much I enjoy them, the cornier and steamier the better.

"Are you having a cozy Saturday afternoon in then?" Poppy asks. I glance around my spare, tidy Bucktown studio apartment. Cozy is not the word I'd use to describe it. I'm hardly ever home, so it has all the personality of an airport hotel. I can't even remember where the framed art on the walls came from.

"Just... getting some work done," I lie, picking up a china teacup off my bedside table and taking a sip of the chilled New Zealand Sauvignon Blanc I poured earlier. It's slightly warm now.

"Look, we're tea twins," Poppy says cheerfully, showing me the cup of tea she's holding. I notice her American accent is softening a bit more every time I talk with her, her crisp California consonants gentled by a hint of a Highland brogue. Although we were raised in the Bay Area with our Scottish dad and American mom, Poppy and I spent every summer when we were growing up with Aunt Ellen at Haye House. Our parents were both ethnomusicology professors at Stanford who used every summer break to do intensive field research. Thankfully they deemed these research trips not suitable for children, and so from the time Poppy was four and I was six until we graduated high school, they would ship us off to Oban to stay with Aunt Ellen. We'd spend the whole summer in Scotland while they studied folk music in remote communities around the world, from tiny villages above the Arctic Circle in Lapland to isolated hill tribes in the jungles of Papua New Guinea.

When Poppy fell in love with Freddie, an Oban local, she moved back to Scotland to be closer to him. They've been inseparable ever since. It's no wonder she now sounds less American than me. Any hint of a Scottish brogue I might have picked up from my time in Scotland has now undoubtedly been erased by the flat vowels of Chicago, my home for the past decade.

"Tea twins." I raise my teacup and pretend to cheers. I don't tell her it is filled with wine. I use Aunt Ellen's favorite floral teacup, but only on Saturdays and never for tea. I haven't drunk tea since I left Scotland. I haven't read anyone's tea leaves either. Somehow it would feel like a sacrilege, even after all this time.

"Do you have a minute to chat?" Poppy asks me, turning serious. "I want to talk to you about something."

"Sure." I glance at the clock. Just past noon on Saturday in Chicago means it's slightly after six p.m. in Scotland. The hour of golden light. For a moment I imagine myself beside her, breathing in the sharp, salty sea air, gazing over the gently rolling hills down toward Oban nestled below. I feel a strange pang of homesickness at the picture. It's been so long since I sat on that stoop in real life. With a sigh I reach for the generously laden cheese plate sitting on my bedside table and carve a generous slice of aged Gouda, placing it carefully on a Nairn's oat cracker.

"Ooh, is that cheese? What kind?" Poppy leans forward and peers into the camera.

"Aged Gouda. I've got five different kinds on this week's cheese plate," I say a touch smugly. My fridge is mostly bare except for an impressive collection of cheeses. It's my one weekly indulgence and the reason I do pilates and barre classes a few times a week to counterbalance it. Every Saturday, no matter where I am in the country, I manage to get my hands on at least a couple of delicious cheeses. Then I settle into bed for a few hours with a good romance novel and a hearty cheese plate. It's my favorite part of the week, my secret, guilty pleasure. I can't imagine anything better to do on a Saturday.

"What are you wearing?" Poppy looks genuinely curious and a little alarmed. "Does that blanket have sleeves?"

I glance down. "It's called a Slanket."

"A what?" she asks, sounding genuinely puzzled. Poppy lives in smart country casual outfits. She perpetually looks like she's in a Polo by Ralph Lauren advertisement. Lots of tailored tweed jackets and cozy cable knit sweaters as though she's ready for a brisk walk over the moors at any time. Today I can see she's wearing an olive-green quilted jacket, English riding breeches, and a pair of black Hunter rain wellies. I don't think it would ever occur to her to wear a blanket with arms.

"It's incredibly comfortable." I explain. "And warm."

This Slanket is the single most comfortable thing I own. It is also the ugliest - a fuzzy polyester blanket with sleeves in a garish red and black plaid. I take it with me everywhere I travel. "You should try it," I tell Poppy, slicing a big wedge off a double cream brie. "It'd be great for all those damp chilly winter evenings."

Scotland specializes in damp, chilly weather and the central heating of Haye House is underwhelming at best. I haven't been back in five years, but I still remember the bone chilling feeling of never being able to get quite warm enough, even during the summers we spent there in our youth. I shiver reflexively and eat my cheese.

Poppy is looking at me with a bemused expression, no doubt trying to figure out how her high-powered, career-minded thirty-two-year-old big sister has been reduced to eating cheese alone while wearing a blanket with arms. I often ask myself the same question. I cast a longing glance toward the book splayed open on the rug below me. I really want to see how Gemma and Laird Lachlan manage to foil each other before finally falling desperately in love.

"I'm calling because Freddie and I have some exciting news," Poppy changes tack abruptly. For a moment I think she's going to announce she's pregnant again, but instead she announces, "We have a chance to buy a microbrewery in Fort William!" She beams at me.

I'm too shocked to say anything, digesting the cheese and

this bombshell of information. Fort William is a historic town in the Scottish Highlands a little more than an hour's drive north from Oban. It's a tourist magnet and has a thriving business district with a strong food and beverage scene.

"You want to buy a brewery?" I squint at her in puzzlement. "Why?"

"You know how Freddie's been taking those brewing courses this past year? Well, he's really been enjoying it, and he seems to have a knack for it," Poppy explains. "A few weeks ago, one of the brewing instructors announced he's selling his brewery and moving to Spain. We went to look at it this week and talk to him. Oh Avery, it's perfect! And he agreed to sell it to us if we want it! Isn't that exciting?" She beams at me.

"Wow, Pops, that's great," I'm trying to process the news. "Does this mean you're going to commute to Fort William?"

That's a long commute to make every day. Plus Freddie and Poppy's twins, Grant and Maeve, just started primary school this year, and Freddie's never lived anywhere but Oban. Their whole lives are centered there. Poppy's eager expression slips a little.

"Well..." she bites her lip. "That's kind of why I was calling..."

Uh oh. I fortify myself with a cube of aged Manchego.

"We're actually thinking of moving to Fort William," Poppy says nervously. She hurries to explain. "The brewery comes with a house on the property, and there's the pub too which we'll need to oversee. It just makes sense to be there. Grant and Maeve have only just started school this year, so they'll transfer schools to Fort William and make friends in no time."

I'm not sure who she's trying to convince more, herself or me. The twins turned six this year. Poppy sends me regular updates – Maeve playing with the circuitry set I got her for Christmas. Grant in his soccer jersey (his football kit as it's

11

called in the UK). He looks so much like dark-haired, pale Freddie, but he has Poppy's freckles. Maeve looks more like Poppy with her bright auburn hair and big brown eyes.

"That's a big change," I tell her thoughtfully. I can see them in Fort William though. Freddie's been interested in brewing for years, and I think they'd be great pub owners. Freddie is level-headed, logical, and has good business sense. Poppy is a social butterfly who never met a stranger. I can actually see this working for them.

"What about Haye House?" I ask the obvious question. Our great-aunt Ellen left Poppy and me the house when she passed suddenly ten years ago. Our father was completely uninterested in the large, slightly down-at-the-heels ancestral pile in Scotland, and since Aunt Ellen never married or had children, we were her closest relatives. In reality, we were closer to her than to our own mother and father. Even though we spent only a few months in Scotland every year, in some fundamental way, it felt more like home to me than our actual home in Palo Alto ever did.

I treasured the freedom of those fleeting months– exploring the quirky nooks and crannies of the ramshackle house, running wild through the moors, and helping Aunt Ellen in her tea shop in town. Every morning felt golden and ripe with promise and possibility and a touch of Highland magic. Those summers were so happy but all too brief. Every September when school began, I'd start a countdown, marking off the days on a paper calendar until we could cross the ocean and be in Scotland again for another magical summer.

"The house, right. That's what I want to talk to you about," Poppy says hesitantly. She twists her hands in front of her and I realize she's nervous. Her flaming auburn hair is plaited in a side braid down her shoulder, and she's gotten a little sun. Her freckles are standing out even more than normal. When I look at her, I don't see a grown woman, a mother of twins, lady of the manor. I see my little sister tagging along to town, begging for a piggy back ride because her legs are shorter than mine.

"We need to sell our share of the house to buy the brewery," she tells me bluntly. "We can't afford it otherwise."

I stare at her for a moment, surprised by the strong twinge of regret I feel at her words. That is nostalgia talking, not common sense. The sooner we sell the house the better.

"Finally!" I set down my teacup of wine. "I've been saying for years we need to get rid of the house."

The manor house may hold many memories, but the taxes are staggering and the upkeep of a house that large and that old is astronomical. It's been a crumbling albatross around our necks for years, but up until this point, Poppy wouldn't hear any talk of selling it. She and Freddie moved in as soon as they were married and have raised their kids there. I honestly thought she might never leave, and so I've been grudgingly holding onto it for her sake for the past ten years. All of a sudden my dream of an early retirement is looking a lot more feasible than I could have imagined. I push away any hesitation. Nostalgia cannot win out over practicality.

"Do you already have a buyer in mind?" I ask briskly.

I picture the cottage I'm dreaming of buying someday on Bainbridge Island in Washington State – a little yellow gabled house with a wide front porch that looks out over Puget Sound. I imagine myself there, curled up by a crackling fireplace with a stack of romance novels and an endless gourmet cheese board while the rain falls softly outside. It's my idea of heaven. Every day would feel like a Saturday.

I stumbled across Bainbridge Island a few years ago while I was closing down a chowder house there. Something about the island captured my imagination – the adorable seaside town, the free art museum, the cool serenity. It reminded me a little of

Oban somehow, in all the best ways. It was the first place I'd been where I could see myself living there. I've been scheming about how to make this dream a reality ever since, and squirreling away money for a down payment every chance I get. Now this opportunity is presenting itself. If we sold the house, surely I could make the dream come true? No more bouncing from place to place, shutting down people's dreams. I could finally make a home somewhere again. The thought is sweet.

I notice Poppy hasn't answered my last question. She's looking off into space, twirling the end of her braid around her finger.

"Pops, do you have a buyer for the house?" I ask again.

I nibble another square of Manchego, wondering how much the house would sell for. I have no idea what the going rate is for Scottish baronial manor houses these days, but surely my half of the sale price would be in the high six figures, maybe more? That means I could afford my dreamy historic little cottage on the bay a lot sooner than I ever expected.

I notice Poppy still hasn't answered the question. Oddly, her face is scrunched up like she's constipated. There's something she's not telling me.

"Spit it out," I tell her. "What is it you're trying not to say?"

She clears her throat. "Um, well the truth is that we're hoping to not sell the *entire* house," she says reluctantly. "We're hoping to sell our *half* of the house. To Cam."

Chapter 3

"Cam. Cameron MacKay?" I stare at Poppy, mouth agape, digesting her words. "You want to sell your half share of the house to Freddie's brother?"

A dozen images tumble through my mind in quick succession. A flash of bright ginger hair and a worn tartan kilt. A pair of warm olive green eyes looking back at me as Cam stands tall and broad shouldered in a damp, misting rain amidst the ruins of an ancient castle. Us laughing and scrambling together over the muddy moors, chasing after Freddy and Poppy. The electric feel of his hand grasping mine as we whirl through the steps of Strip the Willow at the annual Oban summer ceilidh. Me writing *Avery MacKay* in my best high-school cursive over and over in my journal at home in California.

I had a crush on Freddie's older brother through most of high school and anxiously looked forward to seeing him again every summer. As Freddie and Poppy began their own romance, I dared to hope that Cam might feel the same way about me. He worked in a local fish and chips shop in Oban, and I found every excuse to drop in and linger at the counter. He never seemed to mind my visits. When I moved back to Oban after Aunt Ellen's death and my college graduation, I admit I wondered if perhaps something might finally happen between us. By that time, Cameron had gone to culinary school in London and come back home to Oban to work as a sous-chef in the nicest seafood restaurant in town. But then... but then he betrayed me and our family in the most inexplicable, horrible way. I haven't spoken his name for a decade. That man is dead to me.

"You can't be serious." I have no other words for how terrible this idea is. A dozen questions pop into my head, one after the other in rapid fire succession. Can Poppy sell her half share in the house to someone else? Is it even legal? And what does Cameron want with a half share in a crumbling manor house anyway? Do I have any say in this?

But the only question that comes out of my mouth in a bewildered croak is, "Why?"

Poppy hurries to explain. "Cam wants to turn the manor grounds into a working farm and host a farm-to-table restaurant in the manor house. It's a really amazing concept, Aves. He showed us his plans. But he can only afford half the cost of the house, so we're hoping you'll keep your share of the house and be a silent partner with him. That way he can buy us out of our share, we can buy our brewery, the house stays in the family, and Cameron gets to build his business. It's a win for everyone, right?" She flashes a hopeful, tentative smile at me.

My head is swimming with wine and indignation. "Absolutely not," I reply firmly. "That is not a win for me."

"Hear me out, Avery," Poppy pleads. "Cam's idea is really good. And you don't even need to do anything. Cam will be overseeing the property and living on site. You'd get to be a silent partner."

I frown and take a swallow of wine. This is a crazy idea. No amount of cajoling is going to convince me to share a crumbling manor house I do not want and cannot afford with one of my least favorite people on earth. Cameron MacKay is the last man on earth I'd want to do business with. End of story.

"I know you have hard feelings toward Cam because of what happened with the tea shop," Poppy says in an appeasing tone that I find infuriating.

"He helped ruin my life and our family business!" I protest, stuffing a wedge of rich double cream brie into my mouth in distress. "He could have helped me *at* the worst moment of my life and he chose not to. We had to close the business that had been in our family for over a hundred and twenty years. And besides, I don't want to be a silent partner in his restaurant concept. Restaurants are horrible, risky investments," I drive home my point through a mouthful of cheese. "I literally make my living shutting down people's bad restaurant ideas. Roller skating hot dog restaurant... shut down. Tea party on a Ferris wheel where you sit in a giant teacup suspended above the ground and drink tea while you ride? Shut down because of a lawsuit over scalding tea burns. Why should this one be any different?"

Poppy gives me a wheedling look. "You haven't even heard his idea," she coaxes. "Come back to Oban and see for yourself. It's really good."

"No," I balk. "Sell the house to someone else and Cameron can rent it back from them."

Poppy sighs. "What are the odds that a new owner is going to want to let their manor house be used for a farm-to-table restaurant and let the grounds be turned into a working farm? Come on, you know that's highly unlikely. Even if they did, the rent would be astronomical. If he's going to make a go of his idea, Cam needs a partner who already has a share of the house. We'd partner with him, but we need our half of the money for the brewery. You're the best option."

This feels grossly unfair. "I've been wanting to sell the

house for years! I have my own plans and they don't involve the house or Cameron or being a silent partner in anything." I grouse, taking a big swallow of wine. "The answer is no. If you're so bent on this idea, find someone else to buy me out. That way Cameron can go halfsies on the house with a partner who doesn't loathe him."

"But there are things you don't understand about Cam now, factors that I think will sway your opinion." Poppy coaxes. "And you'll like his idea, I promise. Just give him a chance. Come back to Oban and let him tell you his idea. Please. At least talk to him."

"I can't come back," I balk. "I'm the prodigal niece who managed to drive the family business to bankruptcy after a hundred and twenty years, remember?" I empty my teacup and pour more wine into it. I'm really polishing off the bottle at a faster clip than normal. I need to slow down, keep my wits about me. I take another big swallow anyway. Poppy watches me. Her mouth is pinched with all the things she's refraining from saying. She doesn't comment on the wine in a teacup refill either.

"Avery, the tea shop closing was years ago," she says softly instead. "No one remembers that anymore. No one cares. You know you can come home anytime, right?"

I shake my head. "It's not my home anymore, Poppy. I tried coming back five years ago, remember. It was miserable. Everything reminds me of it, of her, of how I messed up and how disappointed she would be."

I know how pathetic I must sound, but it's true. I made a visit to Oban five years ago, and it was as though no time had passed at all. As soon as I set foot in town, I felt like a complete failure. Everywhere I turned I was staring my disgrace in the face once more. And everything reminded me of Aunt Ellen – how much I missed her, how dismayed she would be if she could see how I'd failed to save the beloved business she'd placed in my hands. I cut the visit short by a week and left early, vowing to not return until it stopped hurting. So far that looks like it might be never.

"Maybe this is your chance at redemption, then," Poppy coaxes, her big brown eyes pleading. "I think Aunt Ellen would have loved Cameron's plan. She loved Oban and Haye House. This community and our family heritage were so important to her. Maybe this partnership could be a way to honor her."

"That's a low blow," I mutter. Poppy really knows how to find my weak spots. I feel myself swayed ever so slightly by the mention of redemption, but I'm determined to hold firm.

"I'm not trying to guilt trip you," she says, holding up her hands. "I really think this could be good for everyone. Trust me on this, Avery."

"I'm not interested," I tell her emphatically. "The answer is no. Find someone else to buy the house and see if they want to be partners with Cameron. I'm not the solution here."

Poppy sighs and rubs her forehead like she's got a migraine coming on. "Okay, I'll make you a deal," she offers. "Come back to Oban. If we decide to just sell the entire house to someone who isn't Cameron, you'll have to come back anyway, right? We have to handle the paperwork and divvy up all the furniture and stuff. There's no way around it. So come back and first give Cam a chance to tell you his plan. It's good. It's really good, Avery. And it could be great for our community and our family. If you think is plan is as good as I do, then promise me you'll consider keeping your half share of the house and being partners with him? But if you think his business is a rotten idea for any reason, then we'll sell the house like you want to. We'll just be done with it, okay? You can make the final call."

I waffle. I really want to say no. There is nothing in me that wants to go spend time in Oban. But she's right. I can't expect her to handle everything while I stay safely on this side of the Atlantic. I am going to have to go back to Scotland regardless. And really what is the harm in agreeing to hear Cameron's idea? It's obviously important to her. I'll listen to the plan and then I'll say no. "I get to make the final call?" I clarify.

She nods. "Say you'll come," she urges. "Grant and Maeve want to see you. They're always asking after you. Grant told me last week he thinks you might not really exist, like the Tooth Fairy." She pauses, letting that sink in. I feel a sharp stab of guilt. I've been an absentee aunt, no question about it. I adore the kids, but I haven't seen them in person since they were tiny. FaceTime calls just don't cut it.

I feel my resolve weaken. I've never been able to resist my baby sister for long. I have a lot of vacation time saved up. And I could bump this next job easily. I wasn't all that excited about sports bars in Milwaukee anyway. Maybe going back isn't such a bad idea. I'll hear Cameron's probably terrible and unsustainable restaurant idea, then shoot it down with a little dose of reality and a few solid spreadsheets. Then Poppy and I can sell the albatross of a manor house and I'll be that much closer to my little dream cottage on the Sound. When I think of it that way, going back seems like a pretty good idea.

"Okay," I agree, hacking off a big lump of Gouda and stuffing it in my mouth. "Two weeks. I'll hear Cameron's idea, but if I'm not totally keen on it, we sell the house. Agreed?"

Poppy nods solemnly. "Agreed."

I hold up my pinky. She does the same. We pinky swear, just like when we were kids. I disconnect the call, feeling satisfied. There is no way in the world Cameron MacKay is going to sweep me off my feet. My retirement cottage on Bainbridge Island is virtually a done deal. But first I have to brave going back to Scotland for two weeks.

The thought is sobering. I pour more wine into my teacup,

needing the liquid courage. I can do this, right? I can do anything for two weeks. My mind flashes to Aunt Ellen. She's been gone for a decade now, but she still feels so close to me. At times I turn, half expecting her to be standing there – a tall, rail thin figure with a short blunt blonde bob wearing her favorite hand-knitted oatmeal colored cardigan, sensible loafers, and a patient, wise smile. In my mind she's always holding a teacup brimming with a fragrant Assam or oolong, ready to read the leaves and give me a glimpse of my destiny. Sometimes I talk to her. And not that I would admit this to anyone, but sometimes, every now and then, I swear she talks back to me. Just a whisper, a laugh, a sense of her loving presence.

I sigh. Aunt Ellen would be crushed to see where I've ended up. The future she envisioned for me was in Oban, carrying on our family's legacy, running her beloved tea shop and occasionally reading someone's destiny in the tea leaves, just as the women in our family have done for a century. Just as she taught me to do. Not this lonely existence bouncing from place to place, cutting losses and ending dreams.

"It wasn't supposed to turn out this way," I say aloud to Aunt Ellen, "not according to your tea leaves."

Every summer right before we headed back to the States for school, Aunt Ellen would read our tea leaves. She'd always see lovely things ahead for us– cute boys and good grades, success and adventure. She'd give us something to look forward to as we said our sad goodbyes. But the last time she turned the teacup over and consulted the patterns, the leaves didn't warn her of what was coming. I left to go back to Stanford for my senior year of college with no idea that a sudden fatal aneurysm would take her just a few days before I graduated in the spring. The leaves gave no hint of my hasty return to take over the shop or of what would come, the slow, agonizing falling apart of everything.

"You could have warned me," I say aloud. "Why didn't you warn me?"

There is no answer for a moment, and then I hear it, a whisper soft chuckle and her familiar brogue, a touch rueful. "Sometimes, hen, it's best not to know what's coming."

"Great. Thanks for that," I mutter. "Is this another one of those times? And I making a mistake?"

There is no answer. I sigh in resignation. Aunt Ellen always did whatever she wanted. I see some things haven't changed.

I think about going back to Oban and wonder what I will find there. For a moment I'm tempted to brew a cup of loose leaf tea and see what the future has in store for me. I swirl the wine in my teacup, considering. But then I push the thought away. I haven't read the leaves for years, not since I left Oban. I'm not going to start again now.

Blinking hard, I grab *The Laird's Revenge* and flip to the page where Gemma and Lachlan are waiting for me, locked in a passionate embrace on that cold, windy Highland castle keep. Then I snuggle down in my Slanket, cut a big squishy wedge of brie, drink my third teacup of wine, and try to forget that I just agreed to spend two weeks in the last place on earth I want to be.

Chapter 4

Scotland hasn't changed. After a bumpy flight from Chicago to Glasgow, I catch the train to Oban and doze for three hours as we wind through the high rolling hills and rushing rivers of western Scotland. Everything in April is brown and dun, burnt orange and emerald green under a grey sky.

It's drizzling when I step off the train in Oban mid-afternoon. The feeling of familiarity takes me by surprise. For a moment I stand still on the platform, feeling as though time is accordioning in upon itself. Everything looks the same. Everything smells the same, too. I take a deep lungful of the chilly, salty sea air and feel almost dizzy with remembrance. The cold concrete and metal of the train station mixed with the mouthwatering aroma of grilled seafood drifting from the nearby dock, everything salt tinged with the smell of the sea. I can hear the gulls crying as they swoop over the water of the bay. If I close my eyes, I can almost pretend I'm a child again, ready for summer to begin, the happiest months of my life.

"Avery, yoo-hoo!" I open my eyes, pulled back to the present by the sight of Poppy squelching down the train platform in her wellies, long ponytail flying. She grabs me in a crushing hug, dancing around with me squealing, "I can't believe you're really here!"

I sag in her embrace. It feels so good to be held. It's been so long. She's wearing an orange and green plaid wool coat and she smells like freshly brewed tea and ginger biscuits. She pulls back and gives me a once over.

"Look how skinny you are! So chic and Parisian. But you look a bit peely wally. You need a cuppa. Come on." She grabs my rolling suitcase and gestures for me to follow. Within minutes I find myself tucked into the back of the old yellow Toyota Land Cruiser that Freddie bought in high school. Handsome Freddie, dark hair wind tousled and cheeks ruddy, is at the wheel of the car. He gets out and gives me a peck on the cheek. He is wearing a navy fisherman's sweater and looks every inch a modern Highland country gentleman.

"You alright, Avery? How was your trip?" He asks, his entire demeanor serious and calmly capable, a perfect match for Poppy's flyaway enthusiasm.

"The twins aren't back from a birthday party for a couple of hours yet, so we thought we'd take you up to the house and get you settled in," Poppy explains happily, hopping into the front seat. "They're so excited you're here."

I'm confused. "But I booked a hotel. I'm staying at The Perle."

A room for two weeks at the luxury hotel and spa in Oban had been staggeringly expensive, but seeing as I haven't taken a vacation in forever, I justified the cost. I was looking forward to my deluxe room with a claw foot soaking tub. I figured it would make the visit a lot easier.

Freddie and Poppy exchange a look. "Of course you're not staying at a hotel, silly," Poppy says fondly. "I called The Perle yesterday and cancelled your reservation. You're staying with us at the house." She beams at me.

And just like that, I am back in the small town where everyone knows everyone, where no one minds their own business. I settle back into the seat with a sigh, resigned to my fate. Two weeks. No soaking tub. I could argue, but I know Poppy would take it personally. I can handle anything for two weeks, right? Even staying at the house with all its painful memories?

The drive from town takes only a few minutes, up narrow lanes that climb and curve through the hills. The road is flanked by old stone walls, the pastures rolling down toward the sea in a tapestry of green and brown. In a blink we are pulling into the manor house driveway with a crunch of gravel.

I hop out and gaze up at the house with a rush of nostalgia. Haye House isn't enormous as Scottish baronial manor houses go, but it's still a grand house. I'd guess it's easily twelve thousand square feet. Built from warm, sand colored stone, it boasts numerous tall windows, turrets, parapets, chimneys, and even a tower room. Ivy climbs up one side of the manor, and below the circular drive is a long slope of lawn leading down toward Oban and the sea. The drizzle has cleared and the sun is peeking through wispy grey clouds. As I head toward the front entrance, two large dogs shoot from around the side of the house, barking joyfully. Tongues lolling, they dance around me boisterously.

"Duffy, Daisy, sit!" Poppy orders firmly as she gets out of the Land Cruiser. Both dogs completely ignore her. One, a sleek English Cream Golden Retriever, runs to Poppy. The other, a giant black lab with a goofy expression and a huge, blocky head, rears up on his hind legs and puts his muddy paws on my shoulders, licking me with a long, wet tongue. I shriek and stumble backwards, but he follows me, prancing on his hind legs as though we are waltzing, licking my chin repeatedly.

"Agh! Down, Duffy, stop!" I cry out, trying to fend off his

enthusiastic welcome. Poppy yells a reprimand at the dog, but she and Freddie are unloading the Land Cruiser and cannot rescue me in time. Knocked off balance, I lose my footing and pinwheel my arms, then fall hard onto the muddy edge of the gravel driveway. The dog lands on top of me, his dense weight knocking my breath from my body. "Oof." I groan.

"Duffy, off. Now!" A deep, commanding voice with a low Scottish burr barks out a firm order and the dog instantly obeys, scrambling to attention. Broad hands scoop me up under the armpits as though I'm a toddler who's just taken a tumble. I catch a whiff of good peaty Scotch and yeasty bread and a hint of wood smoke. Flustered and gasping for air, I glance up and up into the startlingly familiar face of Cameron MacKay. For a moment we simply stare at one another. Then Cameron sets me on my feet and steps back, giving me a once over.

"Watch where you're goin' lass, aye?" he tells me with a twinkle in his eye. "We canna have you break in two when you've only just arrived."

"It's Duffy's fault," I protest breathlessly, trying to maintain my dignity while wiping surreptitiously at the mud streaking the seat of my expensive cream-colored silk leisurewear two piece. "He's enormous and very determined." Hearing his name, Duffy wags his tail happily.

This is so not how I imagined my first meeting with Cameron going. I wanted to set the tone, make it clear that this is strictly business and I'm calling the shots. However, that's hard to do when you're bum first in the mud with a giant dog crushing your sternum. My tailbone is throbbing dully, and I'm pretty sure I have mud smeared across my backside in an awkward place. There are definitely two giant paw prints on my shoulders.

Cameron crosses his arms and surveys me with a skeptical expression, giving a noncommittal "hmmph" sound that instantly sets me on edge. "Could be those fancy shoes you're wearing," he points out. I glance down at my pointed, high heeled ankle boots. Not the most practical footwear for the Highlands, it's true.

"It was the dog's fault," I tell him again firmly. "I'm a grown woman. I've been standing on my own two feet just fine for several decades."

"Have you now?" his tone is tinged with skeptical amusement. He raises a ginger brow at my choice of footwear.

I ignore him and opt for what I hope is a dignified silence. Duffy walks over and nudges my hand with his huge head. I relent and give him a scratch under the chin. This entire interaction is not going at all as I hoped it would. I eye Cameron in consternation while he stands there with his arms crossed, looking amused. Seeing him again brings up a welter of emotions – the old spark of attraction mixed with a dull throb of hurt and anger as I recall what he did to us, to me. It's all very confusing.

Cameron may be the most smug and infuriating man I've ever run across, but I'll admit, he is very easy on the eyes. I finally get a good look at him bathed in the pale afternoon sunlight, wearing a tight black t-shirt and a worn kilt in the MacKay tartan, an emerald green and sky-blue plaid design overlaid with black checks. Good Lord the man is handsome. It brings me up short. He's always been handsome, but a decade ago, when I saw him last, he was still growing into himself. Now it's clear he's arrived.

He looks older, but he wears it well. The grooves bracketing his mouth and the hollowed planes beneath his cheekbones suit him, giving him an air of gravitas. I'm tall at 5' 9", and he still towers over me. He's well over six feet and brawny of build, with a full reddish-gold beard and wavy copper hair that sweeps his shoulders. His nose is straight and long, his mouth quirked up in a wry curl, and those eyes – olive green with glints of hazel. They remind me of a Highland burn, of cool water the color of tea from the peat bogs tumbling over mossy rocks. Those eyes send a shiver right through me. He surveys me with frank appreciation and a touch of ironic humor.

"Welcome home, Avery." He nods slightly. "It's been a long time."

"Not long enough," I murmur, giving him a tight smile. Feeling like he has the upper hand irks me. He cocks his head and surveys me as though he's sizing me up. It makes me stand a little taller. Right now I hold all the cards. I hope he realizes that. He has to win me over, and that is a Herculean task because of our history, because of what he did to me.

Involuntarily I smooth my thin silk top, wishing I were wearing one of my power suits, not the "so expensive it looks basic" loungewear I chose for the plane. I want to face off against Cameron in my business best.

"Oh my gosh, are you okay?" Poppy rushes up anxiously with an armload of sports gear including two soccer balls and a cricket bat. "Duffy is a complete menace." She eyes me anxiously, then casts a fond, reproving look at Duffy who is completely unrepentant. Daisy follows at Poppy's heels, wagging her entire back end joyfully.

"You okay, Avery?" Freddie comes up with my carry-on suitcase tucked under one arm. "I couldna get to you in time, but I see Cam came to the rescue." He nods to his brother, then scolds Duffy. "You canna go knockin' over guests, ye great bampot." Duffy woofs happily at the attention.

"I'm fine," I say, a touch grudgingly. I don't want to admit I needed to be rescued by Cameron, but realistically I might still be lying on the ground with Duffy sitting on me otherwise. Freddie goes into the house and Poppy glances between Cameron and me.

"Isn't this great that we're all back together again?" she says in a chipper tone, then sees the look on my face and falters. "Come on, Avery. Let's get you settled. You can shower and change before dinner. It's a special one tonight." She gestures for me to follow her and heads through the giant wooden doors into the house. "Cam's cooking. You're going to love it!"

"We'll see about that," I murmur, loud enough for Cameron to hear me. Then lifting my chin, I brush past him, so close I catch the delicious scent of him again– peaty Scotch and fresh bread and that hint of woodsmoke. I can feel his eyes on me all the way through the door, but I don't look back.

Stepping into the grand wood paneled entrance hall, it hits me all at once, the smell of floor wax and old fireplaces and dusty carpets. "Home," I whisper to myself. I blink hard against a sudden prickle of tears and try to regain my composure. I need a shower and a quiet room and a power suit and maybe a stiff drink. I've only been in Oban for a half-hour and already I am longing for a double Scotch on the rocks. This is shaping up to be a very fraught two weeks.

Chapter 5

I t's the happy cacophony I notice first as I approach the formal dining room after a restorative nap and a quick shower with dubious water pressure. There's a buzzy hum of conversation drifting down the hall with the strains of soft jazz music. I thought this was a family affair, but it sounds like an entire dinner party is in full swing. What in the world is going on?

I peer into the dining room, eyes widening in surprise. The enormous, heavily carved antique dining table can seat sixteen and every seat is filled. Who are all these people?

"Avery, there you are!" Poppy waves to me from her seat near the middle of the long table. She has to pitch her voice loudly over the happy din. I glance around as I make my way to her. The table is simply but beautifully set with candles nestled in arrangements of local flora, the estate's good china and crystal wine goblets. This is a very fancy dinner indeed.

"Auntie Avery!" two high voices cry in unison. My twin nephew and niece jump from their chairs and launch their little bodies across the room towards me with cries of delight. Laughing, I kneel and scoop them into a big hug, kissing their pillowy cheeks. They smell like buttered rolls and bath soap. Utterly delicious. Grant leans back and takes my face in his hands, surveying me gravely.

"You're real," he announces with a touch of awe, as though the tooth fairy has just appeared for dinner. "I dinnae think ye were."

I laugh. "I'm real. What a relief."

I ruffle his hair. He's the spitting image of Freddie except for the smattering of freckles across his nose. He's utterly adorable.

"I knew ye were real," Maeve says confidentially, rolling her eyes at her brother. She has her curly hair scraped back in two little ginger pigtails and has lost her first tooth. She shows me the empty space in her mouth proudly. "I got a pound coin for it," she confides. "I'm savin' ta buy a hamster."

"That sounds exciting," I tell her, admiring the gap where her tooth was. Their Scottish accents are adorably thick.

"Come on, all of you," Poppy calls, gesturing to us. "It's time for the first course." Obediently the kids scamper back to their places. I take the empty seat beside Poppy who is across the table from the children, keeping a watchful eye on them.

"What's going on?" I murmur, sliding into a heavy wooden chair carved with fierce lions. "Who are all these people?"

"It's Cam's supper club," Poppy explains, beaming. "Since he's not officially allowed to operate a restaurant yet until he gets all the inspections and paperwork and things sorted, he's been running a supper club every Saturday night since the fall."

I glance around the table at the other guests. There's a young, wide-eyed couple holding hands and speaking French. They definitely look like tourists. An older, weathered couple in their sixties with sensible sweaters look like locals. I realize with a start that I recognize them. Martha Wilson is a librarian in Oban and her husband Ronnie is a fisherman. A few other faces look familiar too. Across from me the twins are devouring buttered rolls. My stomach gurgles. It's been a long time since the snacks on the train.

"The supper club draws all types of folks," Poppy says. "Locals and tourists alike." She reaches into a wicker basket and takes a roll, splitting it in half and buttering it generously. "The supper club is so popular with locals that often tourists can't get a reservation." She hands the buttered roll to me as though I were a child. It's still warm and smells delicious. "Cam's got a waiting list two months out for these evenings."

Interesting. I glance down the table, noting the diversity of ages and nationalities. That bodes well for Cameron. He's not just attracting one type of diner. I bite into the roll, teeth sinking into pillowy soft perfection, and let out an involuntary groan of satisfaction.

"Glad it meets yer approval," says a voice at my shoulder. I whirl to find Cameron standing behind me, arms crossed, watching my enjoyment with a cool look of interest.

"They're not bad," I say casually, trying to look dignified with my mouth stuffed full of an absolutely heavenly bread roll.

"Good to know," Cameron grins knowingly. "It's my gran's recipe," he tells me. "The secret is buttermilk."

I have a brief mental image of him kneading this dough with those big hands of his and immediately shake it off. Oh no, I don't need to be thinking about Cameron or his hands more than absolutely necessary. I need to keep this strictly professional. I loathe this man, remember? The problem is that for so many years I secretly pined for him before my longing turned to loathing. It's confusing to see him again. It's easier to hate him in the abstract.

I stare at him a moment, then stuff the roll in my mouth and turn back to my plate. Smooth, Avery. Super smooth. Why am I acting so addled around him? What is *wrong* with me? As he moves away, I heave a sigh of relief. Then I help myself to another roll. Whatever my personal feelings about Cameron may be, his dinner rolls are divine.

Around the table everyone seems to be in good spirits. The ostentatious, formal room has a relaxed air tonight that's refreshing. There's a fire crackling in the huge fireplace behind Freddie's chair at the head of the table, and cool jazz background music is wafting from somewhere. A skinny young man in chef's whites with acne and blonde sideburns circles the table pouring wine for the guests. He fills my glass and I take a sip. A crisp dry Riesling. Across from me, the twins are playing a game to see how much butter they can spread on their rolls. So far Grant has piled up curls of butter higher than an inch.

"That's Kenny," Poppy explains, nodding to the young man. "He's Cam's right-hand man. He helps with the gardens and the animals and cooks with Cam in the kitchen." She notices the twins' antics.

"That's enough butter, you rascals! Don't eat it all or Uncle Cam will have to churn more."

I glance at my roll. This butter is homemade? Impressive.

"But I can almost see my roll through the butter still," Grant protests. Poppy fixes him with a quelling look.

At that moment Cameron appears with our first course. He's followed by a slight girl with sleek dark hair pulled back in a high ponytail. She looks like she's around eleven or twelve, with the rounded cheeks but gangly limbs of a girl growing from adolescence to womanhood.

Poppy leans over to me and whispers, "That's Louise, Cam's daughter."

I stare at the young woman in surprise. Cameron has a daughter? How have I never heard about Louise before? I know Poppy carefully avoids talking about Cameron to me, and so I really have no idea what he's been doing this last decade, but Poppy has never mentioned a niece. This seems strange. Also, the girl looks older than ten. Where was she when I was living in Oban a decade ago? Cameron certainly did not have a daughter then.

"How did I not know about Louise?" I ask Poppy, puzzled and intrigued. "Is Cameron married?"

"It's a long story," Poppy sighs, glancing at the twins. "And probably not mine to tell. You'd better ask Cam."

Interesting. Her response makes me wonder what exactly Cameron's life has held in the years since we saw each other. I study Louise with interest. She's dressed in a simple outfit of dark pants and a fitted black top. Even from across the room I can tell she's very pretty, though she looks nothing like Cameron that I can see.

"Welcome to the Haye House Supper Club," Cameron says, standing at the head of the table near Freddie's chair, his broad back to the crackling fire. "I'm your host and chef Cameron MacKay."

I swear every woman at the table sighs audibly. I mean, I get the appeal. He's strikingly handsome, especially dressed as he is. Tonight he's wearing a white double breasted chef's jacket with the sleeves rolled up to reveal his tattoos and his MacKay tartan kilt. I catch a glimpse of the tattoo wrapping around his right biceps, a complex Celtic knot pattern. There's another on his left arm that looks like a Scottish stag. Cameron clears his throat and gives a little introduction to the first course – crostini with cold smoked sea trout and Scottish Crowdie coated in black pepper and dill.

I sit up and listen with interest. I love Crowdie, an ancient Scottish semi-soft cheese that is a distant cousin to the American cottage cheese. Cameron explains the dish and where the ingredients have all come from. Everything is local and he's made the Crowdie and the accompanying crostini from scratch. The sea trout is locally and sustainably caught and smoked. He mentions that Crowdie was probably first introduced to Scotland by the Vikings in the eight-hundreds and that it's thought to be the oldest known Scottish cheese. I watch the presentation critically and am grudgingly impressed by how he carries himself with authority and passion as he discusses the food. This is something he obviously cares about and takes pride in, and it shows.

Cameron and Louise serve the appetizer, placing a small plate in front of each guest. Louise approaches Poppy and me, holding two plates of Crowdie.

"Louise," Poppy says brightly. "I want you to meet my sister, Avery." To me she says, "Avery, this is our niece, Louise."

Louise glances up and meets my gaze. Her eyes are a striking, unusual shade of olive green. I've only seen that color in one other human. Now I can see she's definitely Cameron's daughter.

"Nice to meet you, Louise," I say politely.

She stares at me for a long moment, her gaze direct and a touch challenging, then places a plate in front of me and steps back as though I might bite her. "Nice ta meet you too," she says in a strong Glaswegian accent. Her tone indicates it is anything but a pleasure to meet me. She walks away quickly and I stare after her in surprise. What was that about?

"She knows why you're here," Poppy says in a low tone. "I think she's worried you're going to decide to sell the house."

"Why would it matter to her?" I ask with a frown.

Poppy hesitates. "Louise hasn't had a lot of stability in her life up until she came to live with Cam. I think it would be hard on her if they had to leave Haye House. She loves it here."

"Wait, what do you mean 'leave Haye House'?" I ask in confusion. "Do they live here?"

Poppy nods. "When Cam first came home with Louise, they needed somewhere quiet and cheap to live. We offered them the caretaker's cottage since Arthur and Orla had just moved in with their daughter in Dunbeg. Cam and Louise have been in the cottage for a couple of years now."

I stare at Poppy in consternation. How did I not know this either? Tonight is full of surprises and I have so many questions. I sit back and consider the situation. So not only is Cameron using the house for these supper clubs and seems to have grand designs for the place, he's living on the property as well? I stifle a sigh and reach for my wine. It looks like my time in Oban is destined to be filled with far more of Cameron MacKay than I would like. And now I can add a hostile tween to the mix. This is shaping up to be a jolly visit.

Despite my growing list of questions and concerns, I thoroughly enjoy the appetizer. Cameron is an excellent cook and the Crowdie is the best I've ever had. I finish my entire starter and steal Maeve's. I'm just savoring the last bite when Cameron starts introducing the main dish – a savory Scottish rabbit curry. Louise and Kenny whisk away the appetizer plates and serve the main course. Louise darts a quick look at me as she sets a plate of curry at my place, then scurries away. I glance up to see Cameron watching us. His eyes follow his daughter, and I see a quick, fierce look of protective concern flash across his face. There's a story there, and I wonder what it is.

As we eat the hearty, flavorful Scottish rabbit curry over rice, accompanied by a nicely balanced Beaujolais, the twins chatter excitedly about cricket, some rising pop star in the UK, and Maeve's plans for her future hamster who she has decided to name Pebbles. With her adorable accent, it sounds more like Pay-bles.

We finish the main course and I chat with the single retired woman to my left who is an avid bird watcher and lives in nearby Glencoe.

"I was on the waitlist for two months for this dinner," she

tells me with a look of satisfaction. "And it has been worth every penny. Everyone knows Chef MacKay serves some of the best food in the West Highlands. And he certainly is a braw lad."

She gazes admiringly at Cameron who is standing in the doorway, arms crossed, the picture of stoic calm. I notice Cameron's eyes keep straying to me. I wonder if he's trying to figure out how I feel about the meal. I'll admit I'm impressed by Cameron's cooking skills, but a chef's ability in the kitchen is just one factor in a restaurant's success. There are plenty of other elements that have nothing to do with how the man handles a frying pan. A picture pops into my head of Cameron wielding a frying pan, muscles rippling, perhaps a little sweaty from the heat of the stove...

Stop it, Avery, I scold myself. I've been single too long. I grab my water glass and gulp until it's empty, trying to cool myself down. Just because I've always had a thing for men in kilts doesn't mean I should let myself lower my guard toward Cameron in any way. Yes, the attraction is still there. I'd be a liar not to admit it. But so is the memory of him holding the fate of the teashop in his hands and choosing no mercy. And at the end of the day, he and I want completely opposite things. No amount of homemade Crowdie or those clear olive-green eyes will sway me. I have no intention of giving in to Cameron MacKay.

Louise and Kenny make quick work of clearing the main course away.

"Ooh, look Auntie Avery. It's time for pudding." Grant points and his eyes go round as Cameron rolls a cart into the room filled with parfait glasses. It's the dessert, or pudding, course as it's called in Scotland.

Cameron clears his throat. "Tonight we're serving Tipsy Laird," he explains to the table in his deep baritone burr, holding up the parfait glass. "The Scottish cousin of the English trifle. I've made it with strawberries grown in our greenhouse and soaked the sponge cake in single malt from the Oban Distillery. The cream is from our Highland cow, Enid, who lives a very happy life here at Haye House."

He pauses as the other diners politely applaud. I'm surprised. There is a cow named Enid on the property? There were never any animals here growing up, except for our aunt's crotchety Siamese cat, Pauline. I wonder what else has changed while I've been gone?

The dessert is very pretty, with layers of single-malt-soaked sponge cake, strawberries and strawberry jam (also homemade, Poppy informs me), whipped cream, and custard. Cameron has even made smaller portions for the children without the whisky. I scoop up a spoonful of custard. It's creamy and thick, a lovely pale-yellow hue. Definitely not made with the standard bright yellow Bird's Custard Powder from a tin.

I'm beginning to wonder how this man has time to sleep, what with the handmade butter and jam and custard and cooking dinners for sixteen people. I scoop up another bite and close my eyes in enjoyment, then hear Poppy chuckle beside me. "See, I told you Cam's cooking was amazing." She nudges me. "Are you impressed yet?"

I lick my spoon. "Just because someone can cook doesn't mean he can run a successful restaurant," I point out. "There are at least a dozen metrics you have to consider to determine the viability of a restaurant business concept. Yes, he can cook, and so can most of the chefs in the restaurants I help shut down every day."

Poppy wrinkles her nose. "Oh poo, that sounds so gloomy."

I shrug as I dig my spoon down deep into the trifle glass. Gloomy or not, it's the hard truth. The odds of Cameron's dream restaurant actually being a sustainable business model are low. I know by heart the formulas, metrics, pitfalls, and markers that can mean the difference between a restaurant that will most likely fail and one that has at least a pretty good chance of success. And over the next two weeks, I intend to scrutinize every aspect of Cameron's plans for Haye House until I find a fatal flaw. Then I'll sell this grand old money pit and walk away so much closer to my beach cottage dream. It's as simple as that.

Chapter 6

Late the next morning I stumble down the opulently carved grand staircase from my old bedroom, yawning and groggy from jetlag and in search of caffeine. The kitchen is surprisingly empty. Well, almost empty. The dogs are both dozing in a giant dog bed situated next to the Aga, the large white old fashioned cast iron stove that dominates one side of the kitchen. The kitchen is huge, with a flagstone floor and low, arched stone ceilings, but thanks to the gentle constant heat of the Aga, it has always been the warmest room in the house. It's got a homey feel, despite its cavernous proportions.

Daisy raises her head and woofs a greeting. Duffy whips his tail on the edge of the bed but doesn't even bother to open his eyes.

"Where is everyone?" I ask them, crouching down and scratching them both behind the ears. Despite our rocky start yesterday, I genuinely like dogs. I've always wanted one, but I travel so much I can't have anything more than an air plant. I sigh and get to my feet. It's time for a strong cup of something with caffeine.

"Hi ya, Avery," says a voice behind me. It's warm and deep

and rich with a little ragged edge. I whirl to find Cameron coming out of the walk-in pantry, an apron tied around his kilt and a large bag of flour in his arms. Today he's wearing a dark green thermal shirt under the apron, his ever-present kilt, and a pair of broken-in work boots. I resist the urge to smooth my hands down my thin cashmere sweater and jeans. There's something about his calm, clear gaze that ruffles me. At least this time I'm dressed appropriately for dogs and inclement weather.

"Good morning," I mutter a reply.

"Kettles hot if you care for a cuppa," Cameron says, nodding to the kettle sitting on the Aga. "And there's a fresh bannock if you're hungry." He gestures to a cutting board where a flat, round of bannock is sitting sliced neatly into wedges. "It's just come out of the oven."

A simple unleavened bread made of oat or barley flour, bannock is a popular accompaniment to soup or stew, or an easy snack or breakfast in Scotland. Aunt Ellen used to make it now and then. I haven't had it in years.

"Thanks. Where is everyone?" I ask, making myself a cup of tea with loose leaf tea I find in the pantry, and a splash of milk. I grew up drinking tea the way Aunt Ellen preferred it, good loose leaf tea, none of these tea bags for her. I drink black coffee when I'm in the U.S., but when my feet touch Scottish soil, somehow coffee feels like a sacrilege. Old habits die hard, I guess.

"They're at church this morning, then headin' to Fort William to see about some business with the brewery. They took Louise with them, too. I think they're plannin' to be home later this afternoon. Poppy told me she'd text ye. She felt bad they had to leave before you were up."

I reach for my phone to check my texts, then realize I left it upstairs. I'll get it later. I help myself to a wedge of bannock, skimming it with butter and a little marmalade. I take a bite and find it, unsurprisingly, very good. I wonder idly if there's anything Cameron can't do well. Other than basic human kindness, decency, and friendship, of course.

Idly I watch the pull of his shoulders as he mixes something in a large ceramic bowl with a large wooden spoon. He's less toned than the gym rats I see on my way to pilates or barre class, as though his fitness comes from farm work and not exercise machines and intensive workout regimens. My last boyfriend, Mikael, had graduated from Princeton, was in commodities trading, and looked as though every muscle on his body had been carefully sculpted individually for optimal effect. He was a smart, beautiful, but ultimately sort of boringly self-referential man. I broke up with him eighteen months ago and haven't found someone better since. I've always liked brawny men, ones who feel like they can scoop me up and keep me safe. Cameron looks like he could tuck me against his chest and nothing could ever reach me there.

Oh good heavens. It's too early for this. I chew the bannock and try to think of pragmatic things like spreadsheets. Maybe I need to lay off the Highland romances for awhile, switch to stories with pirates or Navy Seals as the heroes. It's time to take a break from men in kilts.

There is silence in the kitchen except for the scrape of the spoon against the bowl. I take a sip of tea. "So how do you want to do this?" I decide to take the bull by the horns. Best to get this part over with so I can shoot down Cameron's idea and get on with selling the house.

Cameron turns and arches a brow at me questioningly. His hair is pulled back today, and it throws his cheekbones into sharp relief. "I dinnae ken. Do what?"

"I assume you want to tell me your plan at some point if you're trying to convince me to partner with you." I finish off the bannock and reach for another piece, spooning very tasty marmalade onto it. "Let's get on with it."

Cameron narrows his eyes and looks at me for a long moment. I think I've surprised him with my bluntness. "I dinnae want to tell ye," he says finally. "I want to show ye." He wipes his hands on a tea towel. "Come on."

* * *

"This is unfair!" I protest fifteen minutes later. "How am I supposed to resist baby Highland cows?" We are standing outside the Haye House stables in a wash of late morning sunshine, watching a pair of Highland calves totter around their spacious paddock. They're knobby kneed and utterly adorable with shaggy, coppery coats, big brown eyes, and blunt black noses. I reach out and gently stroke one on the muzzle when she sticks her head out through the gate. Cameron leans against the fence, watching me. Daisy and Duffy sit on either side of Cameron, happily wagging their tails and enjoying the day.

"I never promised to play fair," he says, looking amused. I shake my head, all thoughts of profit margins and cash flow melting away under the sheer cuteness of the two calves. A stone's throw away, their mothers watch placidly, chewing their cud.

"Morag gave us a bit of a scare when she calved this little one. I spent a few sleepless nights in the stables with her before and after she had this wee girl, but they're doing great now."

He scratches the small calf's head with obvious affection. I try not to notice how big his hands are and how gently he touches the calf, or how the calf leans into his palm for more. I look away to get my bearings. Swarthy pirates. That's what I need. A good story about a stocky, swarthy, sexy pirate.

I clear my throat. I need to get us back on track and fast.

There is safety in spreadsheets and formulas. I open my mouth to say, "What is the expected prime cost of your proposed concept?" but instead out come the words, "Show me more."

Cameron's smile lights up his face. "With pleasure," he says, and leads the way to the next part of our tour, the dogs following at his heels. In the next paddock we stop to admire a small herd of dairy goats before moving on to meet Enid who is in her own paddock. Cameron explains that she did not calve this year so she can continue to provide milk for making dairy products.

"The animals all serve a purpose here," Cameron explains. "We make all our own butter and some of our own cheese from the cow's and goat's milk."

"You make your own cheese?" I ask disbelievingly. Has Poppy been coaching him on my weaknesses? This hardly seems fair.

"Five different kinds," he confirms. "I'm thinking of experimenting with a blue cheese next."

I shake my head, impressed and slightly nonplussed as we continue the tour. A strapping kilt clad Highlander who makes cheese? It hardly seems fair. Maybe I need a story about a Duke or a Prince. I'm not sure a swarthy pirate is going to cut it after this.

Cameron shows me the old stables which have been updated to make a comfortable indoor living area for the cows and goats. Growing up, this building was all cobwebs and unused bits of machinery. Now it's tidy and bright, with clean straw piled high in the stalls and the faint, not unpleasant whiff of animal manure.

Cameron heads out of the barn into the pale spring sunshine and I follow, taking a deep lungful of the clean air, smelling heather and straw, mud and the sea. Cameron leads me and the dogs in a procession through the herb gardens and newly tilled vegetable beds where tiny lettuces are sprouting and the shoots of snap peas are climbing up trellises. We tour the estate's newly repaired greenhouse where the little green shoots of more than a dozen different types of vegetables are growing. The ground isn't warm enough to plant them outside yet, Cameron tells me. Only the colder weather vegetables can thrive out there right now. I read the labels – courgette, cucumber, tomato, aubergine.

"This is a lot to manage," I observe. "The animals and the gardens and the bread and the cheese making. How do you do it all?"

"Aye, it's a lot of work, but I've got Kenny, the skinny blond bloke from last night," Cameron replies affably. "He's my right-hand man. He studied agriculture and animal husbandry in Aberdeen, and he's been helping manage the animals and gardens and acting as sous-chef on the weekends. He's a good lad and a hard worker." He shrugs. "We manage somehow."

Next up are the chickens.

"We've got a big flock of chickens which supply our eggs and some of our meat." Cameron says as we tour the chicken coop and free-range area for the chickens to wander. We leave the dogs outside the enclosure as Duffy apparently enjoys chasing the chickens, Cameron tells me with a reproving look at the big dog. The large outdoor pen is filled with the sound of contented clucking. "Out on the north meadow I have nine beehives set up. This past summer we harvested our first honey from the bees."

I look around, astonished to see how much has been done on the property. I'm a little annoyed that Poppy didn't think to check with me before allowing all of these changes. I have half-ownership of the house and I had no idea all of this was happening.

"I guess that's what you get when you don't come home for five years," I mutter, rolling my eyes.

Still, despite my grumpiness at not having been consulted about any of this, I have to admit the changes are bringing the estate to life in a way I've never seen before. When Aunt Ellen was living here, it always felt a little empty and echoey, as though its best days were behind it, and we were just living in the shadow of the life it had once held. But now it's bursting with life – chickens contentedly clucking in their pen, calves in the paddock, bees buzzing over the fields, and the tender green plants stretching toward the pale spring sun. I find myself drawn to the life here in a way I didn't expect. My heart yearns for the energy of it, all this building, rising, growing and putting down roots. It all just feels so... brimming with vitality and purpose.

"What do you think so far?" Cameron asks as he leads me down a grassy lane towards his beehives at the north end of the estate. Duffy and Daisy gallop ahead of us, tongues lolling.

"It's a lot of changes from the last time I was home," I say cautiously. "There's so much life now in this old place. It's... refreshing."

Cameron slants a look at me as he falls back to walk side by side with me. "I ken it's probably not that exciting to you. Seein' as you're now a big time consultant, flying all around the States every week. Chickens probably dinnae seem like much to fuss about."

How does he know what I do for a job, I wonder.

He seems to sense the question. "Poppy gives me news about you now and then," he says casually.

Poppy has a tendency to put a positive spin on everything. I wonder what she's told him about me. "My job is not as exciting as it sounds," I assure him dryly. "At least you have cute Highland cows."

He smiles in response. "So what is it that you do?" he asks curiously.

"I help liquidate food-based businesses all over the U.S. I try to make the business closing as painless as possible for the owners and recoup as much of their financial investment as I can."

I don't add that I spend every Saturday alone in a Slanket eating cheese or that I have a suitcase hidden under my bed stuffed full of romance novels. I don't quite know what else to tell him. No kids, no partner, no pets. Do I want all those things? I do, very much. And yet here I am. A decade after leaving Oban, I have a very respectable life - a sturdy 401K, a condo in Chicago. I'm fit and active, intelligent and attractive. I have friends from pilates and barre class and I've joined a rowing club on Sunday afternoons. And yet when I inventory my life, I have to admit I thought there would be more filling my days and giving me purpose by now.

"That sounds like a worthy profession," Cameron observes as he shows me the bees busy around the hives. "Trying to help business owners facing difficult times."

I shrug. "It's a little depressing, to be honest. I'm always the one people come to when things are going really badly. I'm good at handling crises and turning them into opportunities, but it's still hard to see people lose their dreams over and over."

"Do you ever help them save their businesses?" Cameron asks.

I slant him a look. "I'm not that kind of consultant. I'm called in when it's already failed. There's nothing worth saving. I just try to soften the blow as much as I can."

Cameron looks at me thoughtfully but doesn't say anything. I'm relieved. The more I talk about my life, the more aware I am of the scanty measure of it, the lack where I always dreamed there would be plenty. I tuck the thought firmly away. I'm not here to examine my life. I'm here to secure my future. I need to get on with it and stop wanting something more. This is what

47

I've chosen. It's safe, sensible, and minimizes risk. It's everything I've been working toward for so long. Eye on the prize, Avery, I tell myself. Stop wanting what you can't have.

"Tell me your vision for this place," I say abruptly as we head back toward the house. I need to steer this interaction into safer territory, and while I love cute baby cows as much as anyone, I still don't have any idea what Cameron's vision actually is. I promised Poppy I'd at least consider his idea, and the devil is in the details. How will his vision for a business make money? Who will it cater to? These are the things I need to know in order to objectively assess his business proposal. I'm also curious about Louise. Poppy hinted there was a story there. I want to know what it is.

Cameron calls for the dogs who have been sniffing around the hives, then checks his phone which he pulls from a simple leather sporran attached to his kilt. "I've got to tend to my bread dough. I canna let it over proof, ken? Can we head back to the kitchen and talk there?"

I think about conducting a nuts and bolts business conversation while watching Cameron knead bread dough. That seems like a bad idea. I need to not be distracted when talking business.

"Sure." I agree instead, reconciling myself to the fact that I'm never going to say no to watching a man in a kilt knead bread. I just don't possess that kind of superhuman willpower.

Chapter 7

Back in the kitchen, the dogs drink water noisily and then drop onto their bed to nap. I make another cup of tea while Cameron washes his hands at the sink, slips a plain white apron over his head, and then takes the large ceramic bowl of bread dough from the Aga where it's been warming and rising.

"You want me to tell you my vision for this place?" Cameron asks. "It's a bit of a long story, aye?" He looks at me quizzically.

"I have time," I assure him. I'm feeling both curious and a little leery. I'd planned to avoid Cameron as much as possible and here we are chumming around petting cows and making bread. It's hard to reconcile this version of him with the man who betrayed me so deeply a decade ago. The dissonance is unsettling me.

He nods. "Okay then. After culinary school, you remember I worked as a sous-chef at Ship to Shore in town for about a year. Then after you left for the States, I went abroad. I was in Barcelona for a few years, then Stockholm for a year, and Lisbon. All of it working in restaurants, learning all I could.

Eventually I moved to New Zealand and interned at a place called The Priory," Cameron explains, removing the dish towel that he laid over the bowl. "It's just outside of Christchurch, on a historic farm. 'Twas the brainchild of Dominic Warne, the pioneer of the farm to table, sustainable ethos we're using here," Cameron explains, seeing my blank look.

He sprinkles flour onto a large wooden board and turns the dough out of the bowl with a plop. "The Priory is a restaurant, but it's far more than that. It's a celebration of the land and the culture. Everything we served in the restaurant was local to New Zealand. Whatever we could grow ourselves we raised and harvested right there on the farm – pigs, beef, chickens, rabbits, vegetables, herbs, fruits, honey. We baked our own bread and made our own cheese. Dominic worked hard to try to honor local traditions while practicing sustainable and renewable techniques."

Cameron pauses to punch down the dough, kneading it with long, smooth strokes. I make myself keep my eyes on his face. Cameron continues obliviously. "Everything from the garnishes on the plates to the plates themselves to the scraps of leftover food was handled thoughtfully and sustainably," he continues.

"Garnishes," I echo dutifully, trying to focus on what he's saying and not what he's doing with his hands.

"That way of life spoke to me, ye ken" Cameron explains. "I'd worked in tourist traps around Europe, and seen the partying and trash and damage to the ecosystems of so many of these beautiful places. I loved Dom's vision, and how he supported local craftspeople and farmers and foragers."

He pauses to gently oil the smooth dome of bread dough. "About a year into my time there, I realized I didn't just want to be part of Dom's vision, I wanted to build the same thing here in Oban. I started to dream about building my own Scottish version of The Priory, one that celebrated and cared for our own unique heritage and culture and land." He glances at me. "You with me so far?" he asks.

I nod. "Keep going."

He does. "I started really paying attention to everything Dom was doing, learning all I could about what made The Priory so unique. Dominic agreed to mentor me. He knew what I was trying to do and he supported the idea. He took me under his wing and taught me everything I use here now – all the recipes and techniques. I started compiling a book of everything I was gleaning. Here it is."

He wipes his hands on the apron and slides open a kitchen drawer. He hands me a thick plastic binder that must weigh five pounds. I open it and leaf through the contents. It's stuffed full of papers, pages torn from recipe books, and photos. "That wee book is the most valuable thing I own," he says, nodding to the notebook. "It's my blueprint for what I'm trying to build here."

I carefully pick up a handwritten recipe for pickled vegetables.

"I planned to stay for a few years and learn all I could, then try to raise capital and come back to Oban to make a go of it here." Cameron looks at me, his expression resigned. "But then I got the call about Louise."

I have a feeling I'm about to get a lot of answers to my many questions about his daughter. I sit forward eagerly. "What call?"

Cameron squints and massages the back of his neck. "I was... with Louise's mom, Anna, for a few months when I was at culinary school in London," Cameron explains. "We worked together in the same pub in the evenings. She was from Glasgow and just in London for some fun. We were together a few months before she went back home and I finished my course. To be honest, I didn't think much about her after that." He pauses and frowns. "Not until I got the call telling me I had a daughter."

My eyes widen, imagining the scenario.

Cameron continues. "Apparently Anna had been an addict for years and had finally overdosed. Louise was the one who found her mother after the overdose and called emergency services. I don't know how they tracked me down, but I got a call one night while I was on a dinner shift at The Priory. It was from a social worker, asking if I was interested in pursuing custody of my daughter since I was Louise's next of kin." He shook his head in amazement. "I didn't even know she existed, and all of a sudden I discovered I had a nine-year-old daughter halfway around the world."

"Wow," I try to imagine getting that call, how it would turn your world upside down in a heartbeat. Nothing would ever be the same. "And you said yes?"

He nods. "Of course. She needed me," he says simply. "How could I not?"

He gently sets the glob of dough back into the bowl and covers it again. "It was brutal at first, parenting so suddenly. I felt like I was underwater for the first year at least. It was a lot to adjust to. Suddenly back home after almost a decade away and instantly a father to a scared, angry wee lass. I had to start from scratch rebuilding a life for us here." He looks at me, his mouth set in a grim line. "There were days I thought there was no way I was going to make it, but this community really came through for me, for us. Poppy and Freddie offered to let us stay in the caretaker's cottage while I got my feet under me."

He sets the bowl back on the Aga in a spot where it will be warm but not too hot, then comes over and leans on the island across from me. "A few months after I came home, I was trying to figure out what to do. I started to think about the estate and it dawned on me that this is an ideal place for me to try out my idea. The timing wasn't great, and I dinnae have as fleshed out a plan as I'd hoped to or the financial backing I wanted to have. I wasna ready, but sometimes I guess you just have to jump in and figure it out as you go." He spread his hands in a gesture of acceptance. "So here we are. Trying to make a go of it as best we can." His eyes meet mine, and I read in his a vulnerability that surprises me.

"Louise is the best thing that's ever happened to me, but the past few years have not always been easy," he says frankly. "That braw lass has been through a lot in her life. She's a tough wee nut – whip smart and vera sensitive, but she had walls a mile high. She had to build them to protect herself. And I've been working hard to prove myself to her every day since then."

"That sounds like... a lot," I observe. I'm touched by the sincerity in his face. He looks weary and determined.

Cameron nods and blows out a breath. "Aye, it's been bloody hard work. But I wouldna trade one moment of it. She's my world now, and I'm doing all of this for her, too." He gestures out the window toward the stables and chickens and greenhouses. "My dream is still to create a Scottish farm-to-table ecosystem using the ethos of The Priory, but now it's not just my dream, it's for Louise, too. I'm trying to build a sense of place and home she never had. I want to give her that stability, a chance to be part of something that lasts, ken?"

I'm moved by his words despite myself. No matter how unsustainable or misguided Cameron's business idea might turn out to be, I can't fault his motives. It's touching, that he would turn his life inside out for a child he didn't even know existed a few years ago. What a sacrificial thing to do. It speaks highly of his character, which is a problem for me.

It would be easier to say no to him if he were the arrogant jerk I've known him to be, but now I'm seeing a different side of him – Cameron as a hard-working dad trying to make a life and a home for his traumatized daughter. It's softening my feelings toward him in a way that feels dangerous. In business dealings like this, my firm rule is that emotion has no place at the table. That's how you get into big trouble.

I need to remember that, to force myself to look at this situation as I do any other – through a grid of cold, hard facts. There is safety in the system. I need to stick to it now more than ever. Cameron is still going to have to prove to me he's got a rock-solid plan, not just rock-hard abs and a heart-melting backstory. Otherwise he'll have to find some other crumbling baronial manor to turn into his dream come true.

"What's your plan, then?" I ask him, trying to sound businesslike. "You need a plan or else you run the risk of failure. A very high risk of failure."

He slants a look in my direction. "Poppy told me you've got spreadsheets and mathematical formulas, that you live by them. I'll be honest, Avery, I don't have all those numbers for you. I'm sure they're useful, but I don't even know how to come up with some of those calculations. Math was never my strong suit. Numbers cave my head in actually." He scrubs a hand down his face and gives me a rueful look. "All I know is in this book." He taps the binder stuffed with everything he's dreamed about. "I know how to make a damn fine herbed goat cheese and dinner rolls so light they practically float. And I know how to take care of my people, all those that depend on me. I may not have everything you're looking for, but I think I've got an idea that could be a success. Not just financially viable, but good for the land and this community and our family, and maybe even good for you."

He stands across from me, his chin jutted out with a touch of defiance. The overhead lights gild him bronze and gold and copper. I imagine Scottish men have been striking the same pose for thousands of years, stubborn and immovable as rocks.

I understand why Poppy is so enthusiastic about Cameron's

vision. It's a fresh idea that's good in so many ways. Cameron is trying to build something for his daughter while also caring for his community and the land. It's environmental and community stewardship, hospitality and family all rolled into one mouthwatering package. It's a dream he truly believes in, one that he is willing to take a risk for. I understand that feeling. I felt that way once. However it's clear Cameron doesn't know everything he needs to. He's optimistic and unprepared, a lethal combination.

I sigh. I can't believe I'm considering helping him, but for some reason I am. To my great surprise, I have to admit I'm not completely closed to Cameron's idea. Maybe it's hearing about Louise, or maybe it's the baby Highland cows. Whatever the reason, something resonates with me in a way I haven't felt in years. I expected to hear his idea and be able to dismiss it immediately. I mean, this is Cameron we are talking about! What in the world am I even thinking? But surprisingly, I'm willing to give his idea a little more time and consideration. Just a little.

I think of my checklist waiting to be filled in. It's chock full of numbers, ratios, formulas for calculating the probability of success. I need to run the business idea through those formulas, calculate the ratios. A pretty idea can turn into a nightmare that ends in financial ruin and heartbreak. Scores of people learn that lesson every year. I help them clean up the debris when reality hits their pretty dreams. For Louise's sake, I don't want Cam to be one of them, and refuse to tie my interests to some idealistic vision. What worked in New Zealand might not work here. Before I try to parse my own desires and figure out if I am even open to the notion of not selling the house, I have to know this is a rock-solid plan with low risk and a high probability of success.

I stand abruptly. "Get me anything concrete that you have," I tell him briskly. "I'm not promising anything. Nine times out of ten when I run the numbers, it becomes clear that a great idea won't actually work in reality. But I'll at least run the numbers and see what they say."

"Thank you, Avery." I hear the relief in his voice and it makes me feel a little panicked and guilty. I have to remain objective about this. I don't owe him anything. In fact, he owes me hugely, a debt he can never hope to repay. With that thought in mind, I hastily wash my teacup in the sink. I can't believe I'm even willing to engage with him on this. I'm offering him grace he did not offer me all those years ago. But I think of Louise's scared, defiant look at the dinner table. I'll go one step more for Louise. Then we'll see. The numbers don't lie. And while I wait for the information I need, I plan to get a little space from Cameron and his appealing heroic idealism and his damn bread dough. I go upstairs and tuck myself up in bed with a Regency era marriage of convenience romance I brought with me from Chicago. Surely a few hours of scandal with a rakish Duke will set my world and my heart back to rights. Bolstered by this cheering thought, I dry my mug, pat the dogs, and flee.

Chapter 8

Oban looks exactly the same, I reflect as I navigate Aunt Ellen's old red Mini Cooper through the narrow streets of town the next morning in search of good Wi-Fi. The internet at the manor house feels as though it's from the stone age, so here I am, on the hunt for fast internet and maybe a chai latte if I'm lucky.

It's been years since I drove a stick shift, and it's slowly coming back to me. Poppy inherited the Mini from me after I left Oban, and the little car is still miraculously chugging along somehow. I give the steering wheel a fond pat as I rattle along, gritting my teeth against the bone-jarring suspension. I borrowed the car after waking late and finding everyone already gone again. I blame jetlag. It's got me on a weird schedule that is not synchronizing well with the rest of the household. I hardly saw the family yesterday. They were delayed in Oban until suppertime and came home late for a quick bowl of soup and cheese toasties, baths, and bedtime stories which I read to the twins using all the voices. Now I'm on my own for the morning. Apparently Poppy has some sort of moms' meeting at the kids' school about costumes for a school play.

I pull to a stop at a crosswalk and peer around me. Known as the seafood capital of Scotland, Oban is a postcard - perfect charming small town with historic buildings set along picturesque Oban Bay. I drive down George Street with an ache in my chest as the familiar shops and landmarks slide slowly by. There are the ubiquitous souvenir shops all selling the same tartan scarves and lap blankets and hats, a handful of fish and chips shops and a curry house, a store selling local beer and whisky and one selling body products handmade in the Highlands. I find an empty space in a car park and walk back toward a smart new coffee shop I found on Google. It looks like the sort of place that would have a strong internet signal. Maybe I'll get lucky and they'll have a good chai tea too.

The wind is brisk off the ocean, smelling of seafood and salt spray as I head along the water. The sky over Oban Bay is a sullen grey. I burrow into my trench coat, not warm enough for this gusty weather, and walk briskly up George Street. I'm half fearful, half hoping someone will recognize me, but I don't see anyone I know. The street is clogged with clumps of tourists strolling and window shopping and locals dodging them at a brisk pace.

At first glance I think the town is unaltered other than the new coffee shop, but there are other small signs of change. I notice them as I walk by. An old local watering hole has been turned into a sleek looking gastropub. One of the fish and chips shops is gone and is now something called Gelatoburger, whatever that is. I wonder where the Browns are who used to own the chippy. They were always threatening to retire to St. Andrews. Maybe they've finally done it.

Keeping my eyes firmly averted as I near the most familiar storefront of all, I duck into Hinba, the new coffee shop housed in what used to be a pipe and tobacco shop. Inside it is bustling, but miraculously I find an open table for two at the window and sling my laptop bag over a chair back. Settling in with a flat white (recommended to me by the barista instead of their chai), I open my laptop and connect to the internet but don't start working. Instead I sip my single origin brew that is proudly roasted in the "pure Hebredian air" on the Isle of Seil and gaze out the window, trying to ignore the shop on the opposite corner. But it calls to me, siren-like.

With a sigh I give in and let my eyes rest on the oh so familiar royal blue storefront and the paneled white door. It's a whisky and wine shop now, undoubtedly more profitable than tea. I catch a glimpse of a slender blonde-haired woman in the shop and my heart seizes in my chest. For a wild, glad moment I think it's Aunt Ellen. But the woman turns, and I see with a pang of disappointment that she looks nothing like her. I take another sip of coffee, trying to replace the bitter taste of disappointment with the smooth roast. It's hard to see the shop still standing there looking the same on the outside. Inside I know nothing is the same.

The Thistle Tea Room was in our family for five generations, handed down from one generation of women to the next. I was six years old the first time I set foot in it. I fell in love immediately. I loved everything – the cozy, welcoming space with hardwood floors, the smooth plaster walls, and old-fashioned shelves lined with glass jars of exotic loose-leaf teas from around the world. The air was always redolent with jasmine, cinnamon, and the sharp, bitter undernote of dried tea leaves.

Aunt Ellen always treated Poppy and me like we were grown-ups, pouring chamomile tea into delicate real china teacups and adding milk and sugar. I took my first sip and knew I'd found my destiny. It wasn't just the tea I loved, it was the atmosphere, and the patient attention of Aunt Ellen. She brought a sense of serenity that permeated the shop from morning till night, and it quickly became my favorite place in the world. A few years later we discovered that I had the gift. Like Aunt Ellen and the generations of tea shop owners before her, I had a knack for reading the tea leaves. Aunt Ellen took me under her wing and began to teach me all she knew. She would let me sit quietly next to her on a stool as she read the leaves for whoever was seeking advice or understanding. Afterwards she would show me their discarded cups of tea, explaining in detail the shapes and what she'd seen.

"Look at this, Avery," she'd point to the tea leaves stuck to the bottom of the cup. "What do you see?"

Gradually I learned to be able to read the leaves too, to decipher the success promised by the shape of a butterfly, the warning to change course in an X, a promise of good luck in the points of a star. I watched how Aunt Ellen listened carefully to the hopes and dreams and desires of the ones who sought her services. She read the leaves, but she also read the people, trying to use her gift to give them what they longed for - wisdom, direction, assurance. And they loved her for it. She was respected in the community, a woman of integrity, kindness, and empathy. Thinking of her now, I miss her fiercely.

It was not supposed to turn out like this. We had a plan. After I graduated from Stanford, I would move to Oban and we would run the shop together until Aunt Ellen decided to retire. Then I would take over from her. That was what we'd agreed on. Unfortunately a silent, sneaky aneurysm upended our carefully crafted plans. A customer found Aunt Ellen sprawled on the floor amidst shards of glass and scattered thistle tea just a few weeks shy of my college graduation day. She had died instantly. I came back to take over the floundering business as soon as I could, in shock and unprepared. The rest is too painful to dwell on.

Desperate for a distraction, I take my computer from my bag and pull up my email, but then I feel a hand on my shoulder.

"Avery Hayes? Is that really you?"

I peer up into a pair of wide blue eyes in a round, pink face. "Rona?"

"I couldna believe my eyes when I passed by and saw you sitting here," Rona Thomson clasps her hands together in astonishment. "It's been so long since you were back home. What's it been, at least five years?" She clicks her tongue. Rona owns the souvenir shop a few doors down from Hinba. She and Aunt Ellen never did get along, and Aunt Ellen liked almost everyone. A busybody who liked to stir up trouble, was how Aunt Ellen described Rona. She has an angelic face that hides a vicious tongue. Of all the people in town to see me here, Rona would be at the bottom of the list of folks I'd choose. I sigh and give her a weak smile.

"Of course I suppose there's not been so much to draw you back now," she coos, eyes widening sympathetically. "What with the tea shop closing. It must be hard to see it like this, and doing so well." She nods toward the whisky and wine store.

"I'm glad to see it's being kept up," I try to keep my tone light. I just want her to leave me alone so I can bury myself in statistics until this trip is over and I don't have to think about Scotland anymore. Or Cameron. Or bread dough.

"Well it's brave of you to come back. Not everyone is strong enough to face their failures, especially since yours was a family business. How many generations was it in the family before you took it over?" she asks innocently. She's never liked us, feeling like the Hayes were uppity with our big house on the hill above town. It appears that she's still trying to take me down a peg or two. What she doesn't know is that I've got no pegs left to go. I already hit rock bottom when I lost the tea shop.

"So sorry, but I have to take a business call. Good to see you, Rona." I hastily stuff my laptop in my bag, grab my coffee, and hasten out the door. I don't slow down until I'm several blocks away.

On the way back to the Mini, I pass a familiar yarn and craft store. Aunt Ellen's dear friend Annie ran it for decades. On impulse I peer in the window, wondering if I'll see her familiar curly grey head bent over her ever-present knitting needles. Annie isn't in the shop. Instead there is a young woman with thick, straight wheat colored hair pulled back with a clip. She is bent over some sort of craft project with a look of fierce concentration. I start to turn away when she glances up.

"Fiona?" I recognize her instantly. It's Annie's niece. I haven't seen her in ages. Like us, she spent her summers in Oban with her aunt, shipped from her father's latest foreign posting. We'd grown up together having tea parties in the garden and running wild in Dunollie Wood.

"Avery?" Fiona drops her craft project and rushes to the door, her face wreathed in an astonished smile. She was always lovely, and now even more so. "I thought that was you!" She grabs me in a tight hug. "It's been so long but you look exactly the same." She holds me at arm's length, looking delighted. "Come inside. I think it's about to rain, as usual." She pulls a face and ushers me into the shop.

Inside it's cluttered with crafty-items mounded in untidy piles, toppling over, and spilling into the narrow aisles. One wall is filled floor to ceiling with wooden cubbies stuffed with a rainbow of skeins of yarn. It's a chaos of color and textures. I glance around wide-eyed and she laughs and gives me a look of chagrin. "I know, it's a mess. I'm trying to sort through it but it's slow going. Annie wasn't at her best memory-wise in the last few years, and things got pretty bad. Dementia." She frowns. "You should see her house! This is small potatoes compared to that mess."

"Oh, I'm sorry...is she..." I hesitate.

"Gone a month now," Fiona says with a wobbly smile. "I flew back for the funeral and somehow I'm still here. I thought it was just going to be for a week or so, just to get things squared away, but it looks like maybe I'm staying longer now." She bites her lip and looks unsure. It feels like there's a story there. One she may not be ready to tell me just yet.

She brightens. "What are you doing in town?" she asks.

"Figuring out if we're going to sell the house or not," I tell her. "Poppy and her family are moving to Fort William. They're buying a brewery."

"Good for them!" Fiona says. "That sounds like an adventure. Still, it will be sad to see the old place go if you do sell. I have such fond memories of it."

"So do I, but I'm based in Chicago now and with Poppy moving to Fort William, it just doesn't make sense to keep it."

Fiona shakes her head. "Ah time. Doesn't it seem like a blink ago that we were ten and your aunt was reading our fortunes in the tea leaves?" She looks nostalgic, a far off look in her eyes as though she's peering back in time.

"It does," I agree. I glance down at the counter by the register, at what she was working on when I peered in the window. It's difficult to tell what it is. A lumpy orange knitted object that might be a pumpkin or maybe a spaceship?

"You want to know something ironic?" Fiona asks, seeing my confused expression over her misshapen craft project. "Annie left me her craft store and I'm absolutely rubbish at crafts." She puts her hands on her hips and shakes her head. "I keep hoping I'll get better with practice but so far no luck." She quickly tucks the ugly knitting project away under the counter. "Is it weird to be back in town?" she asks, changing the subject. "After... everything that happened." She hesitates and I know she means the tea shop. I'm sure she heard all about it from Annie or another town citizen. It was big news at the time.

"A little," I confess, meaning a lot. "It's been a decade since the shop closed, but it feels like people think of it like it was yesterday." I sigh. Already I'm weary of bearing the weight of history. Anywhere else in the world I'm just Avery Hayes, hot shot liquidation consultant. Here, everything is laden with layers of complicated history. Even me.

Fiona nods glumly. "I know what you mean. I've lived all over the world, but it's like all those years don't matter. Everyone still thinks of me as Annie's young niece. A shop-keeper in town called me "wee Fiona" the other day and I'm thirty-three! There's a way that this place feels stuck in time."

I nod in agreement. I have the feeling that no matter how old I get, I'll always be Ellen's screw up niece. It's a depressing thought. My phone dings with a text. Poppy, wondering where I am.

"Fi, it's great to see you," I tell her honestly, "but I've got to run."

"How long are you in town?" she asks eagerly. "Want to grab a pint and catch up before you leave?" She walks me to the door, dodging precarious piles of merchandise as we go.

"I'd love to," I tell her. We exchange numbers and a last hug, then I duck out the door and head for my car.

I walk along the street until I reach a quiet, empty section of sidewalk, then lean over the stone wall and stare out at the bay. Who am I kidding? For a moment I got carried away with the allure of Cameron's dream, but this visit to town has brought me firmly back to reality. I think of my nasty interaction with Rona, of what Fiona said about this place being trapped in time. It makes me feel panicky, like I can never live down or outrun my mistakes here. This is why I've stayed away. This is why I didn't want to come back. Because no matter how long it's been, a town this small never forgets. And I cannot forget either. I will be a failure in Oban until the day I die. Nothing can change that. It's time to cut my losses and get out of here, I decide. I'm more than ready. I've been ready for a decade.

I pull out my phone and dial a number before I can change my mind.

"Amir? It's Avery."

Amir Hassan is an old college boyfriend of mine. We dated for a few months before deciding that we were better as friends. Now we grab dinner together any time I come through L.A. Amir is a high-powered real estate broker.specializing in luxury properties around the world. He's the person I need right now.

"Avery!" Amir crows, sounding happy to hear from me and maybe a little tipsy. I can hear pulsing music thudding in the background like he's at a party or club. I check the time and realize it's very late in L.A. I didn't calculate the time difference before I called. "Sorry to call so late." I apologize.

"I never sleep, you know that." Amir says airily. "Tell me you're in L.A. Want me to send a car for you?"

"I'm not even close to L.A.," I respond with a sigh. "I'm in Scotland. Tell me, Amir, do you have any buyers who are interested in a seaside Scottish manor house?"

Chapter 9

"You took the Mini to town?" Poppy chirps when I get back from Oban and find her in the kitchen, enjoying a cuppa with a plate of tea biscuits and cucumber sandwiches in front of her. There's a cup of tea waiting for me too, perfectly brewed. Poppy doesn't have the gift of reading tea leaves like I do, but Aunt Ellen taught her to make a fine cup of tea. There is no sign of Cameron anywhere, for which I'm grateful. "Was it a walk down memory lane?" Poppy asks, motioning for me to come sit with her.

"Something like that," I mutter, tossing the keys to the Mini in the bowl where I found them this morning, lying amidst a pile of single keys, pound coins, a whistle, and a dog leash. The dogs are curled up in their giant bed beside the Aga, snoring.

"What happened?" Poppy asks, reading my mood.

"Rona Thomson saw me in the coffee shop in town and did her usual thing." I slide into the chair at the kitchen table beside Poppy.

"Rona Thomson is a gossiping biddy who likes to stir the pot," Poppy frowns. "Whatever she said, don't listen to her."

"The problem is, she isn't wrong." I sigh. "She just

reminded me of why I never come back here. No matter what I do, no matter how successful I am in business or who I've become after all these years, I'll still just be the Hayes girl who torpedoed her family's tea shop." I reach over and snatch a custard cream cookie and take a bite. It was always my favorite tea biscuit when I was a kid.

"Some people may think that way," Poppy says comfortingly, nudging the plate of biscuits closer to me. "But most people can look past it. Lots of folks are new in town too, and won't know anything about what happened in the past. I think you'd be surprised by how few people remember, and even fewer care."

"Maybe, but it sure doesn't feel like it." I shrug, stirring milk into my tea and taking a welcome sip. "I saw Fiona, by the way. Did you know she's back? She's taken over Annie's shop which looks like a yarn bomb exploded in it. It was great to see her. She said she's having a similar experience, feeling stuck in the past."

"Maybe the problem isn't that other people won't forget what happened," Poppy says delicately, nibbling on a Jammie Dodger. "Maybe the problem is that you can't forgive yourself for it."

I snort but can't come up with a good reply. She's right. I haven't forgiven myself. How do you forgive yourself for failing your family and the woman you respected most in all the world? I have no idea how to do that.

Poppy changes tack. "What did I miss yesterday?" she asks, eyes wide and guileless. "Did you talk to Cam?"

I get the feeling she already knows that I talked to Cam.

"I got to pet adorable baby cows and we talked about his vision for the farm, yes." I confirm, selecting a cucumber sandwich from the plate and biting into it. It's buttered on both sides, just like Aunt Ellen used to make.

"And..." Poppy prompts, leaning forward a little too eagerly.

"And nothing," I shrug. "It's an appealing idea, but he's not prepared. You can't have a pie in the sky dream and expect it to work out. These things take meticulous planning, data, analysis. As far as I can tell, he's done none of that. I'm not even sure he knows how much he doesn't know."

"But you do," Poppy says conversationally, but there's a crafty look in her eye.

I sense a trap somehow and proceed cautiously. "I have a pretty good grasp on what makes a food-based business successful, yes."

"So you could help him." She makes it sound so logical.

"Maybe, I say calmly, finishing my sandwich and selecting a chocolate bourbon biscuit. I really need to stop eating these. Cameron's baking is already providing enough temptation. I want to still be able to button my jeans when I fly home. I eat the cookie anyway.

Poppy looks crushed. "I thought when you got here, when you heard his plan and saw what he's done with the place, when you met Louise and heard how he's trying to build a life for her..." Poppy stops, her voice quavering. "I thought when you got home and saw the twins again...you'd change your mind."

"Poppy, I left this place for a good reason," I say as gently as I can. "I don't plan on coming back. And I want fewer things tying me here, not more."

Poppy looks hurt. "But we're here. Your family is here."

"I know," I say even more gently. "And I love you all. I really do. I just can't stay connected so closely to somewhere where I'm seen as a failure, where I can't ever outlive a dumb mistake I made when I was twenty-two. In Chicago, I get to be the version of me I created, that I decided I wanted to be. Here I'll always be Ellen Haye's daft niece, the one who destroyed the family business a year after inheriting it. It's humiliating and it hurts and there's nothing I can do to get past it. So I choose to stay away. It's just easier that way."

Poppy sniffs and looks down at her tea. "Easier for you," she murmurs. "We really miss you. I miss you. I want you to know my kids. They're amazing little humans and they're growing so fast. I don't want you to blink and realize you missed it, that they're grown. I don't want you to be all by yourself in Chicago, so focused on your career that you realize one day you missed all the good stuff in life too."

I hear the truth in her words and it stings a little. I don't admit it, but I worry about that too. That I'll miss all the good stuff and at the end of my life all I will have to show is a string of failed businesses I helped to liquidate, a lonely condo, a pilled Slanket and cheese board, and a suitcase stuffed full of romance novels. It's a thoroughly depressing thought. But there has to be another alternative than throwing my weight and financial security behind a probably-doomed business concept with a man I've hated for a decade in a town I want to avoid as much as possible. There must be a better option.

"I told Cameron I'd run the numbers," I concede, mostly to placate her. "We'll see what they say."

I glance outside and notice sun peeking from behind the clouds. That reminds me, I have work to do while the light is good. "I'll come visit you in Fort William as soon as you're settled. Maybe at the holidays?" I offer.

She thins her lips and squints at me suspiciously, but she lets the topic drop.

"I'm going to stretch my legs," I tell her. "Take a walk down memory lane." I feel a little guilty not telling her what I'm actually up to, but I don't want to muddy the waters until I have something concrete to talk over with her.

"Okay, well I've got to figure out how to make a costume that looks like a pancreas for Maeve. Their school play is anatomical this year." Poppy rolls her eyes. "Grant is a thumb. There are no patterns for body parts, so I'm just going to have to wing it."

She stands and grabs the plate of biscuits, heading for the pantry. I snag an oaty Hobnob biscuit as she walks by and then take out my phone and head for the front hall. Today I am taking matters into my own hands regarding the future of the manor house. Step one was calling Amir. Now for step two.

* * *

Step two is taking photos of the house and property for Amir. He texted me on my drive home from Oban to say he already has a few potential buyers in mind and would I please send some photos and information about the house. I feel a little panicky about the speed at which this is going. I'm not ready. The house isn't ready. Hence the impromptu photo session. I need to get ready... and fast.

Walking through the house and grounds is like stepping back in time. Everywhere I look I see poignant reminders of my childhood. I wander into the dusty library and for one heart-stopping moment I think I see Aunt Ellen sitting there on the slouchy, broken in leather club sofa, her favorite wool throw tucked over her legs, a steaming teacup nearby. She looks up and smiles at me, patting the worn seat beside her. "Come sit by the fire, lammy" she invites, her brogue thick and warm as treacle. "Grab yourself a book. What do you fancy this evening – murder or love?"

When I blink, of course the sofa is empty, but I can picture her so vividly. That sofa is where we would all three curl up on rainy evenings and read in front of a cheery but inadequate fire Aunt Ellen built in the huge, drafty fireplace. When we were little she would read to us as we sat tucked against her side like chicks under a hen's wings. Later, when we were older, we'd all still gravitate to the sofa and each read our own books in companionable silence, munching tart apples from the overgrown orchard in the south meadow and drinking cocoa or tea. I run my fingers over the rows and rows of books on the shelves–some ancestral tomes mixed in with Patricia Cornwell and Agatha Christie. Aunt Ellen loved a good murder mystery novel.

Upstairs I bypass the threadbare grandeur of Aunt Ellen's old bedroom suite which is now Poppy and Freddie's room, not wanting to invade their privacy, and skip the twins' bedrooms as well. I'm staying in the room Poppy and I shared as children, at the end of the long hall. Inside, I snap a few photos - the twin canopy beds, the faded Persian carpet, and the sweeping views out the windows. The room looks out over the slightly unkempt formal garden. The hedges need a trim, I notice. If you crane your neck you can catch a glimpse of the sea shimmering silver far beyond. I open the window and stick my head out, searching for a glimpse of copper curls and gold pigtails playing hide and seek in the hedges. I can still hear the echo of Poppy and me as children, laughing and chattering as we raced into the house for tea and biscuits, wind-blown by the cold sea air and speckled with mud.

In the bathroom, I turn the taps on the huge antique cast iron tub. The water is tinted ever so slightly brown, like very weak tea. I take a photo of the tub and bathroom with its antique charm. What pictures don't show is how drafty the room is. Facing the sea, this room always seems to have a sharp wind whistling through the single-paned mullioned windows. I shiver, remembering years of bath times where the boiler could not warm the water enough to keep up with the chill.

"It's so cold, Avery, hurry!" I hear Poppy's high little voice, teeth chattering as we raced to see who could dry off and slip into their flannel nightgown faster.

Despite the myriad inconveniences of living in a drafty, ancient house, we adored our time here. We loved it all - the house, the tea shop, the freedom to run wild, and the warm care of Aunt Ellen. Our home in Palo Alto was a stable, peaceful one, and our parents loved us in their slightly distracted way, but we knew we always came second to their work. All school year as we were shuttled to and from school and taken to a variety of enriching after-school activities by nannies, we counted down to June and the promise of another golden, tantalizing summer of freedom and fun.

I look around the bathroom and sigh. How long ago that all seems now. How I wish I could go back, even just for a day. The nostalgia surprises me. I've spent so many years trying to ignore everything about Scotland that I'd forgotten how much good there was here, how loved and happy I felt. It's bittersweet, the remembrance, tainted by what came after. I draw a deep breath, trying to bring myself back in the present as I quickly tour the rest of the house, snapping photos in each room, but everywhere I look I keep catching a flash of blonde braids and copper curls and hear Poppy's and my high, childish giggles drifting from around every corner.

Trying to shake off the intense wave of nostalgia, I head outside and walk the length of the circular driveway in front of the house, snapping a few photos of the impressive façade. Then I turn to take in the panoramic view. The day is fresh and sunny, with a light salty wind off the bay. I take a few pictures of the bucolic setting, the gentle hills rolling away from the manor down toward Oban and the sea, the pastures outlined by low stone walls and dotted with copses of trees. Far out in the bay the low green mound of the Isle of Kerrera rises from the water and further still, against the horizon, sits the Isle of Mull.

"Now that's a braw view, isn't it, hen?" I whirl, startled by Aunt Ellen's voice in my ear, sure I'll find her standing beside me, wearing her old brown wellies, her egg yolk-yellow mackintosh and a satisfied expression. She always swore this was the finest view in Western Scotland and by that score, the world. I can't say I disagree.

Finding the driveway empty, I drink in the view with a sigh. Once I thought I would never leave this place, that it would be my home forever, and I would be buried next to Aunt Ellen in the church yard in town and rest forever in the soil of Scotland. How things change. I have nowhere like this in my life now, no place that feels like home. Our parents sold the Palo Alto house when they retired five years ago. Now they live in a small town in Mexico and are always traveling. When I spoke to them last, they were headed to South America for a few months to spend time recording the traditional music of a small group of Indigenous people in Uruguay. California never felt as much like home to me as Scotland anyway, so the loss of our childhood home did not sting much. But being back in Scotland feels... painfully conflicted.

Feeling restless and unsettled, I pause to send the photos to Amir. As I do so, I wonder if I'm making a mistake, yet another in a long line of them. But what is the alternative? It makes no sense to keep this house. And what would it accomplish? I cannot turn back time and redo my mistakes. What's done is done. Even if this house does hold a handful of happy memories, they are overshadowed by my feelings of regret and failure and the shame of knowing what my actions cost my family. Best to be rid of it then and just move on. With an irritable shrug, I head inside, trying to convince myself to do just that.

Chapter 10

"Oh sorry, just looking for a cup of tea," I stop in surprise in the doorway to the kitchen late the next morning, feeling like I'm interrupting something. Cameron is standing at the island chopping herbs and Kenny is at the stove stirring something in a big metal pot. Both are wearing white aprons over their clothes. The air is warm and thick with steam and the smell of milk and a sharp tang I can't identify. No one else is around. Poppy sent me a panicked text this morning telling me she had to drive to Fort William to buy fabric for the ill-fated anatomy costumes. The kids are at school and Freddie is consulting with lawyers about the brewery sale today.

Cameron glances up and for a startled moment his pupils flare in surprise, but then he says calmly, "Hello, Avery." With his delicious accent it sounds like "haloo."

"Hi," I say as nonchalantly as possible, rounding the island. "Don't mind me. I'm just here for some toast."

I'm suddenly glad I took the time to dress in jeans and boots and a short-sleeved sprigged blouse instead of just coming down in my pajamas. I was up late last night and slept late this morning. My conversation with Amir, running into Rona and Fiona, and my chat with Poppy all kept replaying in my mind. Not even a rakish duke could distract me. I found myself reading the same chapter over and over, unable to concentrate on the main characters' scandalously passionate embrace in the orangery. Finally I gave up and took an Ambien. Now I'm tired, groggy, and feel like my nerves are stripped raw. I need tea and toast and maybe a dram of whisky.

Cameron nods toward the pantry. "There are some dinner rolls left over from the supper club. Help yourself. Or there's sourdough bread if you prefer. Word to the wise, I'd avoid using the toaster though. It burns everything to a crisp."

He gestures toward an ancient looking toaster plugged in on the counter near the sink. It looks like the same toaster Aunt Ellen had when we were growing up, and it seemed old back then. Dinner rolls it is. I head to the pantry and come back with two rolls and a crock of homemade butter. If my luck holds, maybe I can find some of Cameron's marmalade, too. For someone I purport to detest, I have to admit that I'm thoroughly enjoying Cameron's skills in the kitchen.

Kenny bobs his head at me deferentially as I pass the stove. "What are you making?" I ask him as he stirs a huge white blob of something in a murky liquid.

"Burrata," Cameron answers from the island. He has his big plastic binder open on the island and is consulting a hand-written recipe.

I freeze. "You're making cheese?" Burrata is definitely in my top five favorite cheeses in the world. I peer into the pot with interest. My mouth waters thinking about that creamy goodness smeared on one of Cameron's rolls.

"Want to help us?" Cameron offers calmly. I hesitate. I could just take my rolls to my room and get some work done, but the temptation proves to be too great.

"I'd love to," I abandon the rolls and butter and instead go stand next to Cameron, eyeing the recipe written in a bold, square hand. Breakfast can wait. The air around him smells like parsley and lemon thyme as he finishes chopping herbs.

"Kenny's making the burrata, and I'm finishing up the goat cheese we started two days ago. It's been sitting in the molds in the refrigerator firming up and now it's ready," Cameron explains. He goes to the refrigerator and comes back with a tray containing twelve small cylindrical plastic containers filled with a white substance. He sets the tray down and hands me an apron, helping me tie it in the back. His fingers brush the nape of my neck and I shiver involuntarily.

"Do you want to help me finish the goat cheese?" he asks and I nod eagerly. I can't remember the last time I was so excited to try something new.

"Turn the basket over on this waxed paper and tap it like this." Cameron gives the bottom of the little plastic cylinder a hard tap and the white substance inside falls out with a neat plop. He lifts away the basket to reveal a lovely round of soft goat cheese with a pretty basket weave pattern pressed into it from the container.

"Ooh, it's lovely," I bend down and examine it. "I'm a little obsessed with cheese," I admit, straightening up.

He smiles, one corner of his mouth curling up in amusement. "Poppy may have mentioned that."

I turn to him with a mock frown. "Is this a setup then? Are you trying to sway my opinion?" I can't really be mad because I'm just so excited to be making cheese.

"No, we make cheese every month," he assures me. "Just a happy accident you came in."

He shows me how to gently roll a round of goat cheese in cracked pepper to make a pepper coating. Some we leave plain and some we coat in herbs. Two he finishes with a coating of lemon zest and spoons blueberry jam on the top.

I'm completely absorbed by what we're doing, focusing hard on obeying Cameron's instructions and doing it right. It's painstaking work to treat the cheese gently enough and not damage it, and I feel a thrill of triumph when I roll the last one in fresh herbs and set it carefully on the tray.

"Well done," Cameron says approvingly, and I feel a flush of pride. I'm around restaurants all the time, but I'm always tearing things down, never creating. It feels good to create. If you had told me last week that I'd be making cheese under the tutelage of Cameron MacKay, I would have told you that you were crazy. Yet here we are. Of course I still loathe him and blame him for his ruthless actions, but something happened yesterday, something shifted as he talked about Louise and his dream for the farm. I was reminded of the Cameron I knew before the betrayal, the Cameron I pined over for years with good reason.

"Burrata's ready," Kenny calls from across the kitchen, then glances at me and blushes pink so fiercely it looks like he's been broiled alive. I get the feeling he may not be around women much.

"You want to learn how to shape the burrata?" Cameron invites and I agree without even hesitating. As Kenny tidies up the kitchen, Cameron takes me to the big pot on the stove and shows me how to pinch off a fist sized piece of burrata and mold it into a smooth sphere. As I watch, his big hands deftly poke a hole in the ball of cheese and carefully stretch the mozzarella to make a little coin purse sized bag. He shows me how to stuff the cheese purse with a delectable mixture of frayed bits of mozzarella combined with cream, spooning it from a waiting bowl. Then he twists and pinches the cheese purse closed, leaving a perfectly round, glossy ball of burrata that holds a delicious secret inside. I'm eager to try my hand at it, but it's harder than it looks to get the technique right.

I pinch off too much cheese, and then too little, and each time Cameron patiently corrects me, showing me again how big each ball should be. I feel like a total novice, frustrated by my lack of skill. Cameron is patient though, and soon I'm laughing at my own clumsiness and trying again. On my third attempt I nail it, and carefully form the little purse, though I accidentally stuff it a little too full of the creamy filling. I manage to twist the top closed though, and whoop when I'm finished, holding my little burrata aloft like it's a precious work of art. Cameron watches my enthusiasm with a look of amusement.

"You've got the knack for it," he tells me, shaping the burrata with brisk efficiency. "It took me weeks to figure that out."

Pleased by the compliment, I eagerly reach to shape another ball and then another and another. When I glance up, it's been almost an hour and I've lost track of time. I've been so thoroughly enjoying the work that I didn't even notice the minutes flying by. I glance over at the plastic tub of whey sitting on the island, filled with happy little burratas bobbing around. Looking at our handiwork, I feel a sense of supreme satisfaction. How long has it been since I put my efforts toward making something, not tearing it down in the most cost-efficient way possible? For a brief moment I wonder what it would feel like to spend my life doing things that feel productive and enjoyable. I can't remember the last time I did work that felt like play.

Just then my stomach growls so loudly Kenny hears it from across the kitchen. He darts a quick look of alarm at me.

"I'll clean up here and then water the seedlings," he says.

"Thanks, Kenny." Cameron shuts the plastic binder and carefully replaces it in its drawer. "Now for the last step," he says to me with a twinkle in his eye. "We taste what we've made."

"Quality control. Good idea," I agree briskly, trying to quell the hungry gurgle of my stomach. Cameron gathers a plate of rolls, a sharp knife, one of the goat cheeses with lemon zest and blueberries, and a ball of burrata, and nods to the refrigerator.

"Can you grab us two Irn Brus?" he asks. "And do you prefer inside or outside?"

"Outside," I respond promptly and follow him out the door, drinks in hand.

Chapter 11

"Are you okay sitting in the garden?" Cameron calls back over his shoulder as he exits the kitchen and heads toward the shabby formal garden at the side of the house.

"Sure, that's great." I follow him, holding the bottle of Irn Bru, the iconic bright orange soda that is beloved all over Scotland. I've never had Irn Bru for breakfast before, but then again I've never eaten cheese I've made with my own hands before, or shared breakfast in the sun with my crush turned grudge, so there is a first time for everything.

We settle on the wide stone steps leading from the side of the house to the gravel paths of the formal rose garden, now sadly overgrown. Poppy and I used to play Barbies on these steps, acting out Cinderella fleeing the ball or dramatic scenes from Roman mythology. I sit down next to a large stone planter holding a boxwood topiary in need of a trim. The view from here is stellar, looking out over Oban and the bay, and the sunshine brings a welcome warmth to the chilly stones. Aunt Ellen loved this rose garden and tended the dozens of rose bushes with care.

Now it's fallen into neglect. The leggy canes of the roses are not yet in bloom, though they have green leaves in profusion. The only sounds are bees buzzing industriously and the twittering of birds. The sun is warm on the stones and I stretch like a cat, grateful for the heat. I set the bottle of Irn Bru between us.

"I could only find the one big bottle," I tell Cameron apologetically. He shrugs and grabs the bottle, untwisting the cap. "I don't mind sharing," he says, "Do you?"

I shake my head, crossing my arms over my knees and gazing over the vista. Cameron offers me the bottle first, and I take a small sip, wishing it were tea. The fruity, sweet fizzy drink tastes like nothing else in the world. Honestly I've never really cared for it. I hand the bottle to Cameron and he takes a drink. I watch the long lines of his throat. There's a grace to his movements, as though every action is intentional. He takes up exactly the space he intends to and moves through the world with purpose.

He slices open a roll and smears some of the fresh goat cheese on it, then hands it to me. The flavor is creamy and tangy and the blueberries and lemon zest are a tasty surprise.

"Wow that's good." I close my eyes and savor it. "If you're trying to tempt me into keeping the house, this is a strong start," I tell Cameron, mouth full. I regret the words almost immediately, but his mouth quirks up in amusement.

"Is it working?" he asks. He eats his half of a roll in two big bites.

"No," I tell him honestly. The mood instantly sobers.

He turns, resting his hands on his knees and watches me curiously. "Can I ask why not?" he asks evenly.

"Because I don't have any interest in keeping the house," I explain. "I've been trying to convince Poppy to sell this place for years. It's bleeding money. And I don't have any intention of coming back to Oban or being tied to Scotland, not if I can help it."

He looks at me, brow furrowed in puzzlement. "I thought you loved this place," he says quietly. "I remember when you came back after Ellen died. You said you were planning to stay here for the rest of your life."

So he does remember that horrible Oban Preservation Society meeting. So do I.

"That was before," I say shortly.

"Before what?" He cuts into the soft rind of the burrata which gives under his knife like ripe fruit splitting open. Cream oozes out and my mouth waters.

"Before the Preservation Society denied my request for help, and I lost our family business," I say bluntly.

"Ah," he looks at me in understanding, those clear olive-green eyes searching my face. "So all of this is about Ellen's tea shop then?"

"What else?" I shrug, looking away. It's still painful to talk about it. "How could I stay after I took the business generations of my family built and ran it into the ground?"

Cameron lays down the knife. "Is that why you've stayed away all these years? Because of the tea shop?" he looks surprised.

"Of course!" I burst out. "How could I stay? I was constantly reminded of my mistakes everywhere I turned. People's memories are long here. I felt like everyone saw me as a failure. They couldn't forget and neither could I. So I left." I reach down and brush at a few flecks of lemon zest that have fallen into my lap. My appetite has suddenly vanished.

"Did you ever think that you might have done the right thing when you closed the tea shop?" Cameron asks almost casually. He picks the knife back up and slices the last roll into quarters.

"What do you mean?" I look at him out of the corner of my eye.

"Was the tea shop on solid financial footing when Ellen died?" Cameron asks. He scoops some of the creamy burrata onto a piece of roll and offers it to me. I take it reluctantly.

"Well... no. I mean, things had been tight for a while." I admit. "There had been a steady decline in the profits for a few years before she died. The place was struggling."

In reality the books had been worse than I thought when I finally got my hands on them after her death. They'd been such a tangled mess I couldn't make heads nor tails of them no matter how hard I tried. I'd had a panic attack the first night trying to unravel everything and failing miserably. I'd realized that everything was now on my shoulders, that I had to somehow rescue this mess. It felt utterly overwhelming - too sudden and too much. That feeling never went away until the day I closed the tea shop doors for good. Then the panic was replaced by a crushing feeling of guilt.

"So why do you think you're to blame for the shop closing?" he asks, mouth full of roll.

"Because I should have been able to save it," I tell him shortly. "And maybe I could have if the Oban Preservation Society had approved my request for an emergency hardship grant. But they didn't, and you cast the deciding vote."

"I remember," he says quietly. "I've always wondered if you blamed me for that decision. I understand why you do."

"How could I not?" I can't keep the quavering note of anger from my voice. "Your dad was down with pneumonia that night and so he sent you to vote in his place. I asked the Preservation Society for help, for a hardship grant that would have bought me a little more time to get things sorted out and make the business profitable again. It was a split vote, half the Society members for and half against. Your vote decided the matter. And you voted no. I had to close the shop the next week and sell everything off to pay the debts." I hear the note of bitterness in my tone. I can't help it.

The memory of Cameron's young, serious face as he broke the tie, how he wouldn't meet my eyes as he cast his vote, still makes me burn. He could have offered grace and he chose not to. And the cost of his decision tore my future apart. I've never understood why he did that to us, to me. He was supposed to be my friend.

Cameron is still staring at me. "Avery," His tone is serious. "Look at me."

Reluctantly, I do. I'm flushed and angry and humiliated, remembering it again. He held my future and my family's business for generations in his hands and he chose to deny us mercy.

"Avery," Cameron says softly, his gaze serious. "Listen to me. The tea shop was doomed no matter what. It had been struggling for years. Ellen had come to the Preservation Society twice before asking for a hardship grant to help cover her expenses. Did she tell you that?"

"What?" I'm shocked and taken aback by this information. "No, she never mentioned it to me." I stare at him in chagrin. Surely that can't be right. She would have told me, wouldn't she? Why would she keep that from me?

"The grants are supposed to be kept highly confidential which is why no one on the Society committee could tell you why they voted no. But it's been a decade now since then, and Ellen has passed, and I think you not knowing has done more harm than good." He frowns. "My dad was the head of the Preservation Society when they granted Ellen's request...both times," Cameron says. "The second time she asked, they told her if the business couldn't sustain itself, she'd need to close it.

They made it clear that they couldna give her any more help. The hardship budget can only stretch so far. There were other businesses who needed funds too, and it's bad for the entire business community to keep a business alive that canna turn a profit." He leans forward intently. "Ye ken what I'm sayin' Avery? That's why when you asked again, we said no. My father instructed me to say no because the committee had already said yes twice before."

I stare at him for a moment in stunned silence. In light of this new information, the Preservation Society's reluctance to help made more sense. But why had Aunt Ellen never mentioned it to me. Had she felt ashamed?

"I had no idea," I tell him. "Even so, I was supposed to be able to save it," I murmur plaintively. "I thought I could save it."

""Aye," he says sympathetically, reaching over and placing his big, warm hand over mine. "But you were set up from the start to fail, ye ken. You inherited a lame horse. The tea shop couldna keep itself going even when Ellen was alive. It was only a matter of time before it folded. If Ellen had lived a few more months or years, she would have been forced to make the same decision you did. It was just bad luck that you had to take over when it did." He gives my hand a squeeze. "No one could have saved it. Even if you'd managed to prop it up for a bit again, the future wasna looking good. Increased operating costs, rising property taxes. And the shop wasna bringin' in much money. People's tastes change. Tea shops are not as popular as they used to be. It's hard to sell enough tea to make a living, no matter how long your family's run the business. That tea shop had run its course. It was just a matter of time before it ended one way or the other."

I sit for a moment, absorbing his words. I'm acutely aware of his hand on mine. There is comfort in that touch from the most unlikely of sources. I've hated this man for so many years, and blamed him for so callously destroying my dream. And now in the space of a few minutes, I am seeing the past in a different light.

What if Cameron is right? What if the tea shop was doomed to fail regardless of who was at the helm? I spent plenty of anxious nights pouring over the costs and revenue columns, trying desperately to make the numbers work. I blamed myself when they didn't, when I finally had to admit defeat. The memory still stings – the humiliation and helplessness I felt. But what if I was wrong to place the burden of blame directly on my shoulders? Well, on my shoulders and on Cameron's as well? What if neither of us was at fault?

This changes everything...

Cameron clears his throat and gently removes his hand. "I know you dinnae like me," he says. "And I know I'm probably the last person you'd want to go into business with..."

I wince because it's true. "Did Poppy tell you that?"

He grins and arches a brow. "Poppy doesn't have to tell me anything," he said. "When you look at me, you have an expression like you're biting into an unripe quince, all sour and suspicious."

I flush, caught out. He's not wrong though.

"I was a bit worried you've been plotting my murder all these long years," Cameron jokes.

"Jailhouse orange isn't my best color," I deadpan.

He laughs. "That isna true. You'd look bonny in a paper bag, Avery." He sobers and clears his throat, looking a little self-conscious. It's the first time I've seen him flustered about anything and it's sort of endearing, now that I realize maybe I don't have such solid cause to hate his guts. "If you decide to sell the house or not, of course it's your decision to make," Cameron says, and I realize he's nervous. I sit up and pay closer attention.

"If you dinnae want to work with me, I understand," he

looks down at his hands, loosely laced over his bent knees. "But I'm hoping you dinnae decide to sell the house because of a grudge about something that happened so long ago." He shoots me a quick look. "And if you're selling because you're scared to have roots here and you're haunted by something that wasn't your fault, I think you should reconsider. It's time to let that go." He looks out over the garden to the bay and says frankly. "All I'm asking is that you make your decision wisely, Avery, considering all the facts. Because a lot hangs on this decision for me and for Louise."

"I know," I tell him softly. For the first time when I look at him, I don't feel that sick sensation of resentment and grief. And when I think of the tea shop, it feels different too, as though the guilt has lessened. What a relief.

He nods. "I'm not trying to guilt-trip you, Avery. You're a savvy businesswoman. I'm sure you can find any number of things wrong with my plan. But if there's something you like about it, if there's something that appeals to you, please at least consider it. It would..." He looks away and clears his throat. I get the feeling he's not used to humbling himself this way and it's uncomfortable for him. "It would mean a lot to me and to Louise if you would at least give us a fair shake."

I don't say anything for a long minute, considering his request. The decision is a complex one, tangled up in history and my own issues and hopes for the future. Now with this new information from Cameron, I'm not sure how I feel about anything. I need to let it settle.

"I can't promise the outcome you want, Cameron," I tell him finally. "But I can promise to give you a fair shake. I've seen a lot of businesses start and fail and I've got a very good nose for trouble. I won't say yes unless I truly think it's an excellent idea with real promise to succeed. There are potentially a lot of reasons for me to say no."

He nods. "Aye, I know." He pauses and then asks almost shyly. "But are there any reasons for you to say yes?"

I think about it, eyeing the cheese and the gorgeous, single man sitting next to me. He could not have designed a more appealing picture if he'd tried. "Maybe a few," I concede.

There is no way in the world I'd ever admit that Cameron is growing on me, or that this morning he may have slid from the list of negatives to the list of reasons I might possibly be inclined to say yes. How can I help but be swayed? It's the cheese. I blame the kilt and the excellent cheese.

"That's a start then," Cameron says, smiling in relief. He scoops up a generous portion of burrata and smears it on the last quarter of roll, then hands it to me. I drop my eyes at the fizzy feeling I get when his fingers brush mine, like my blood is suddenly carbonated. I need to be very, very careful. Now that I realize my resentment toward him all these years wasn't really justified, I am suddenly aware of just how much there is about him to like. And that is dangerous. Emotions cloud judgement. They're risky. And I don't do risky.

"You have to stop feeding me like this," I chide him with a groan. "I'm going to have to buy new trousers at this rate." But I take a bite anyway.

He grins, completely unrepentant. "So what if you go back to America plump as a wee hen? Let someone take care of you for a change, Avery," he says gently. "I get the feeling it's been a long time since anyone did."

I clear my throat and look out at the sea, focusing on a distant ship as I chew. His words trickle through me, sweet as golden syrup. They touch a tender, lonely place in my heart. How long has it been since someone took care of me, even to make me a cup of tea, let alone feed me cheese on delicious rolls they made by hand?

I try not to think about the suitcase under my bed and the

fact that Cameron looks uncomfortably similar to some of the men posing on the cover, shirtless in kilts amidst heather covered moors. I wonder for a moment what he would taste like if I leaned over and kissed him, and shiver as I imagine him pressing that firm mouth against mine. I feel like a teenager again, as though I might go upstairs and write *Avery MacKay* in my journal over and over.

I stuff the rest of the roll in my mouth, choke on a crumb, and start coughing.

"You alright?" Cameron asks in concern, thumping me on the back in a decidedly unromantic way. It does the trick and brings me back to reality.

"I'm okay," I wave him off, wheezing a little. I grab the bottle of Irn Bru and take a gulp. Time to put some distance between me and this walking enticement before I'm tempted to do something foolish.

"I'd better get some work done," I tell him lightly, standing and avoiding his eyes. "Thank you for the cheese making tutorial. And the enlightening conversation."

"Any time." He stands too, holding the plate of crumbs. "Avery," his tone is serious. I meet his eyes, his own searching and holding mine.

"It grieved us all when Ellen died so suddenly," he says finally. "You weren't ready to take on the responsibilities of running the family business, but you tried. Everyone knows you did everything to save it. Be kind to your younger self, aye? You did the best you could, and that's all anyone can ask of another person."

I can't swallow around the sudden knot in my throat. I just blink hard and nod, then turn and beat a hasty retreat. I don't come down for the rest of the day.

Chapter 12

"**A**unt Avery, you landed on Mayfair again," Maeve crows, holding out her hand. "You owe me fifty pounds."

"Again?" I sigh and pay up, wondering just how I've ended up playing Monopoly with the world's most real estate savvy six-year-old. I was supposed to just have a quick bowl of soup in the dining room with the family, but then Grant and Maeve pleaded for one game before bed.

It mushroomed from there, with Freddie lighting a fire in the fireplace in the most comfortably shabby of the sitting rooms, the one near the kitchen that Aunt Ellen had always favored. Her old floral print armchair is still drawn up to the fire, and Poppy sits there working on a crossword puzzle. Freddie is sprawled out on the sofa, checking the rugby scores. There's big band music playing on an old radio in the corner, broadcasting some sort of BBC Scotland program. The dogs are snoozing in front of the fire and the entire vibe is cozy and warm, smelling of wood smoke and furniture polish and a hint of dusty upholstery. I'm sitting with the twins at a card table in chairs we've brought in from the kitchen.

It was my idea to play Monopoly after I spotted our beloved childhood Monopoly set in the wardrobe in our old bedroom. Poppy, Aunt Ellen, and I had spent hours playing Monopoly in the evenings as Aunt Ellen listened to BBC on the radio and we sucked on squares of sweet, buttery homemade Scottish tablet – a classic Scottish confection with a slightly harder, grainier texture than fudge. Poppy always wanted to be the dog and I always chose the ship, "so I could sail to Scotland any time I wanted to."

The twins, as it turns out, are Monopoly novices, but while Grant mostly just likes to pass Go and collect two hundred pounds, Maeve revels in her role as a real estate mogul. She's smart and ruthless and reminds me, a touch disconcertingly, of myself.

Grant rolls the dice and moves the top hat. "I'm buying King's Cross Station," he announces, forking over two hundred pounds of Monopoly money to Maeve who is the banker. I planned to work on more house information to send to Amir this evening, but I have to admit that this is more fun. Last time I saw the twins in person they were toddlers. Now they're fascinating little people with very different personalities. Maeve is organized, bossy, and take-charge, a mini-CEO in the making. Grant is warm and silly and quick to tears. I find myself utterly charmed by them both, and make a promise to myself that I won't wait so long to come back to visit. After my chat with Cameron this morning, I'm finding the thought of coming back to Scotland far more palatable. I didn't know how much his words would release me from the hold of the past.

Just then there is a distant sound of knocking from the direction of the kitchen. The dogs jump up and go crazy, barking and running into the kitchen.

"That'll be Cam," Freddie says calmly, glancing up from his phone. "He said he might stop by."

A moment later, the barking stops and I hear the deep tones of a familiar voice calling a greeting.

"Hallo the house," Cameron calls out.

My heart gives a strange little thump, and I almost miscount on my turn and end up on the Go to Jail space until Maeve corrects me and places my ship on the yellow Piccadilly space instead.

"Pay attention, Auntie Avery," she tells me sternly. I nod obediently.

"We're in here," Poppy calls back and Cameron pops his head into the room. Behind him I see Louise peering at us hesitantly.

"Anyone care for a cuppa?" Cameron asks, tossing a leather satchel on a chair by the door. "I'll put the kettle on."

We all agree, and he disappears into the kitchen. The dogs flop back down in front of the fire with long-suffering sighs, and Louise hovers in the doorway.

"Louise, you can come play with us if you want," Maeve offers. "We've only just started a second time around the board. You wouldna be much behind."

Louise slides her eyes to me, then nods. "Aye, thank ye," she agrees. She sits down across from me and tucks her legs under her, giving me a quick look from under her dark lashes. I think of what Cameron told me of her upbringing. What a strong young woman she's had to be, growing up too soon with no one to care for her until she found Cameron and this wonderful family. My heart aches a little for her for those lost years, although I'm glad she's here now.

"You can be the horse," Grant tells her, putting the figurine on the Go square. Maeve hands her the initial amount of money and the twins agree she can have three turns in a row to help her catch up.

Cameron returns with four mugs of tea. He's made it how I

like it, I realize in surprise, with no sugar and a splash of milk. And he's used good loose leaf tea, not the normal tea bags.

"Thanks, this is perfect." I bury my nose and inhale the fragrant steam. His eyes crinkle as he smiles, taking a sip from his own mug. He's wearing a kilt and a dark green shirt that brings out the bottle green flecks in his eyes.

"I remember you drink it like Ellen did. She always said sugar spoiled the essence of the leaves."

"That's right, she did." I'm surprised he remembered. He's brought snacks with him too, a packet of prawn crisps and a handful of Tunnocks tea cakes. I unwrap one and bite into it, instantly transporting back twenty years by the soft marshmallow and chocolate treat.

Cameron goes to the satchel he dropped on the chair and takes something out of it. "The information you asked for," he murmurs, coming back over to me. "For my proposal." He taps the folder. "It's not complete, but it's all I've got at the moment. Projections and market analysis and that sort of thing. Let me know if you need anything more." He hands it to me.

"Thanks. I'll take a look," I say, trying to be cool and neutral despite what my pulse is doing at his nearness. I take the folder from him and Cameron goes to sit next to Freddie on the sofa. A minute later they're arguing about rugby. I try to tune them out and turn back to the board, but since this morning, I seem to have developed a radar for Cameron. I'm intensely aware of his every move out of the corner of my eye. Great. I really don't need an ill-timed return of my high school crush to muddle my decision.

"Come on, Hayes. Keep it together," I murmur.

We play for a few more minutes, the twins bickering about the rules and Louise playing referee and reading the yellowed rule pamphlet to settle the argument.

"Animal named for both the color of its fur and for its

habit?" Poppy asks aloud, pencil poised over the crossword. She's always loved crosswords. Aunt Ellen used to get her a book of them for her birthday every year. "Louise, you like animals? Any ideas?"

Loiuse shakes her head. "Ah dinnae ken," she says, then hesitates and offers, "maybe a wee sand cat?" She rolls the dice and moves three spaces, landing on the Electric Company which she buys.

"Louise knows everything about animals," Maeve confides to me. "Did ya ken that an earthworm has ten hearts? Louise told us that."

"Sand cat is correct!" Poppy cries jubilantly from the armchair.

I sip my tea and look around me. It's been years since I was in such a cozy domestic scene. I glance at my sister who is penciling in an answer, the pink tip of her tongue stuck out the side of her mouth. Freddie and Cameron are good naturedly bickering about their rival rugby clubs. The dogs are snoring, tails thumping as they enjoy a happy dream. The fire crackles and pops, and I take another swallow of tea. Around the card table, the twins are in a heated discussion about buying houses, and Louise is consulting the rule book again.

I can't remember the last time I was out with this many people in the evening. Sometimes I meet up with a work colleague for a drink after work, or go see a concert or a play with a few of the women from my barre studio when I'm in town. But most evenings I'm alone, curled up in my Slanket, chapters into my latest romance novel. I think of the half finished one tucked away in my suitcase. I could slip away from this game now that Louise is here, raid the kitchen for some of Cameron's burrata and tuck myself in bed upstairs. It's tempting. I love my routine. I entertain the thought for a moment, but strangely it's lost its allure. Unexpectedly, I have found myself in the center of this very ordinary domestic scene, and I find I'm enjoying it. I've missed these types of evenings without even realizing it.

"Aunt Avery, it's your turn again." I glance back at the board to find all eyes on me. Grant holds out the dice.

"Right. Sorry." Chastened, I take the dice and roll a four, landing on Whitechapel Road. I buy it, and then another thought stops me in my tracks. This happy domestic scene depends on me. If I decide we should sell the house, tonight may be the last time we all gather like this, together in this room. I glance around with fresh eyes, feeling the weight of that decision settle heavily on my shoulders.

The choice I make will affect not just me, but everyone sitting here. If I sell, the twins will not have a family home to inherit. They will not bring their children into these ancestral halls. I glance across the table at Louise and find her staring at me, her dark eyes studying me with a narrow expression that straddles the line between fascination and fear. She meets my gaze, unblinking, and I read in hers a challenge. She has a soft, sweet face, but there is nothing soft in those eyes. They look older than her years, and wary. I think of Cameron and Poppy explaining the harsh circumstances of her early life. I flick a glance at Cameron who is arguing with Freddie over a bad referee call in the game. My decision will cost Louise and Cameron the most if I choose to sell.

And yet if I do not, I open myself up to so much risk, so much potential failure. If I partner with Cameron and keep the house, I will give up the dream of a cottage on Bainbridge Island for a long time. If I keep the house, it will be years and years before I can afford to buy my cottage. The thought is sobering. Suddenly every swallow of tea tastes bitter in my mouth. I'm facing a decision with significant consequences no matter what I choose. And unfortunately I have no idea which way to go.

* * *

Early the next morning I tiptoe through the house to the kitchen, hair pulled back in a ponytail and running shoes in hand. Only the dogs are up, and they greet me with soft whuffs and wagging tails. I lace up my shoes and let myself out the kitchen door quietly, picking up my pace as I round the house on the gravel path. At the end of the drive, I take a left hand turn and wind up the hill on a narrow road with stone walls that hug the gentle curves. I'm in pretty good shape, but the steep hills are far more of a challenge than my usual treadmill workout in whatever hotel I'm staying in that week. I draw deep lungfuls of briny air, enjoying pushing my body to its max.

One mile, then two, and three. I'm feeling the burn of exertion, letting my thoughts sift and settle as the ground falls away beneath my pounding feet. I'm tired but feel wired, as though every sense is elevated, every nerve ending laid raw. It's jetlag and being home and the conversation yesterday with Cameron. My mind keeps circling back to our talk in the rose garden, to the compassionate look on his face when he told me about Aunt Ellen and the hardship grants. I'm not used to being the recipient of looks like that, of people seeing my soft underbelly. But I trust Cameron and surprisingly, I find I'm actually glad. How astonishing to find that he is not the villain in this story after all.

I stop to catch my breath on a bend in the road, the manor house far below. Farther still are the dark rooftops of Oban and then beyond the shining silver sea. I think again of what Cameron told me, about the tea shop's precarious financial position and slow decline. I've been turning our conversation over in my mind since yesterday. It seems clear to me now I didn't fail the tea shop. It was already failing, and I simply could not do enough to save it. There is sadness in the realization, but relief too. Enormous relief. It was not my mistakes or poor management that bankrupted it. It was simply too far gone to save.

"I'm sorry I couldn't save it," I murmur to Aunt Ellen, imagining her standing beside me in her wellies and yellow macintosh. "I tried my best. It just wasn't good enough."

"I'm sorry I left it in such a sorry state for you, hen," I hear the echo of her voice. For the first time I wonder if the stress of struggling and failing to turn the tea shop's fortunes around was too much for her, if her aneurysm was a result of carrying that load for so long. We'll never know, but I suspect it might be true. I know that stress well. I carried it from the moment I learned of her death until the day I shut the doors for good. And since then I've carried a different heavy load – one of shame and guilt and feelings of failure. But now what do I have to be ashamed of? What have I been running from all this time and why?

My cell phone rings, startling me. I answer, still trying to catch my breath.

"Hello?"

"Avery? You sound winded. Are you being pursued by wild beasts out there in the far reaches of Scotland?"

"Hi, Amir. Nice to hear your voice too," I say dryly. "What's up?" I start walking back toward the house.

"I have some clients who are potentially interested in buying your manor house," Amir says bluntly.

My heart thumps in my chest. That was fast. "Really? Who are they?"

"Business folks based in LA. He's in land development and she owns a skin care company. They've been looking for a family estate in Europe. I guess she's a fan of some historical time traveling TV show set in Scotland. They're interested in seeing the house. If they like it, they're in a position to make an immediate offer." Amir sounds proud of finding potential buyers so soon.

"Wow." I hesitate. I'd anticipated I'd have more time. This feels so sudden.

"They want to see it as soon as possible. There's a chateau in France they are looking at, too. The wife is also a fan of *Emily in Paris*. They want to come see both houses and make their decision soon. I think they're leaning toward Scotland, so if you give them a nudge, we could seal the deal," Amir confides.

"How much are they willing to pay?" I ask. We haven't even talked about price. I have no idea about price.

"That's for you to work out by the time we get there," Amir tells me. "For the right house, they're willing to pay a pretty penny. So pull out all the stops. A word of advice; they want to feel like they're buying a piece of history. You need to show them whatever passes for a good time in Scotland – tea and tartans and whatever else you have to offer. Just no haggis, okay?"

"Right, okay. Pull out all the stops. No haggis. I can do that." I stare down at the house far below. It sits serenely in the early morning grey light, the turrets poking up over the brow of the hill. I feel a strange sort of reluctance when I think of these potential buyers setting foot there, but I shake off the feeling. I need to keep my options open. I try to summon a vision of the little cottage on Liberty Bay, but I can't quite manage it.

"We'll be flying into Glasgow and hiring a car," Amir announces. "They want to come to see you after they see the chateau in France, so we'll arrive on Sunday."

"In four days?" I squeak.

"You asked me to find buyers for you," Amir says, a note of impatience creeping into his voice. "These people are perfect. They're loaded and eager and money is no object. If they like it, we can have your house under contract almost immediately." He pauses expectantly.

"You are a miracle worker, Amir ," I reply weakly. I know that's what he wants to hear, and honestly, it's true. It's not his fault I'm suddenly getting cold feet. What is wrong with me?

"I am," he preens, then blows me an air kiss over the phone. "We'll see you Sunday. Wear your best tartan for us, darling."

Chapter 13

I spend Thursday and Friday avoiding everyone as much as possible while doing market research on the house and pouring over Cameron's proposal. Amir's call lit a fire under me. This is all moving so fast. I thought I'd have more time to decide. But now it appears I have only a few days to make my decision. So now I need to crunch numbers and assess risks. It's time to get serious about the realities of this house and two very different futures that lie before it. I've got a huge decision to make and very little time to make it.

"You're like a ghost. We never see you anymore," Poppy complains when I pop downstairs Thursday evening to grab a bowl of stew and make some slightly burned toast. Cameron is right: the ancient toaster burns everything.

"I'm reviewing Cameron's proposal," I tell her, which is true. I don't mention what else I'm doing. Poppy has made it perfectly clear that she wants to sell their half of the house to Cameron and have me become his business partner. I know she'd frown on the idea of Amir and his buyers if she knew about them, so I don't tell her.

"How's the proposal looking?" Poppy asks eagerly. "Is it good news?"

"Too early to tell."

I allow myself to be cajoled by the twins into a game of Monopoly before their bedtime, Maeve trounces us all again, then I shut myself away with my computer.

It takes time to run a full analysis on Cameron's business idea, especially because I have to fill in a lot of blanks myself. He hasn't given me everything I need, but it's enough to at least begin to make some sort of a projection about how viable his business idea is. I spend hours researching restaurants in the area, looking at things like price points, cost of doing business, and rate of failure for restaurants in Oban.

The picture that begins to emerge is inconclusive. Since Oban is a tourist town, there is definitely a higher-than-average demand for restaurants which is good news. Costs are high in the UK in general though, which is bad. There are no other restaurants on the west coast within a hundred miles that offer the same sort of experience Cameron is wanting to provide, which can be both good and bad. Good because it's unique, bad because diners are not necessarily familiar with or seeking out what he will offer. Cameron and his team will have to build a reputation and that takes time.

By the time I'm finished on Friday, I've used as many metrics as I can to calculate prime cost, overhead rate, average gross profit margin, net profit margin, and a list of other factors. Unfortunately, I'm still stumped. Cameron's business proposal has more merit than I originally thought, but it's still a definite risk. And if I say yes to partnering with him and choose to keep the house, I assume some of that risk myself. Risk makes me nervous. The thought of watching another business slowly fail and go under makes me queasy.

Prudence would dictate that we sell the house now while

the market is good and we have interested buyers. Poppy and Freddie can take their half and buy their brewery. I can take my half and buy my cottage. Cameron can approach the new buyers and make a business proposal or find another place to set up his farm and restaurant. Easy peasy, clean and simple. There is absolutely no good reason on paper for me to take the risk on Cameron's business and let a perfectly good offer from buyers slip through my fingers. And yet... and yet. I find myself hesitating over the numbers, looking for ways to make saying yes to Cameron make more sense. This is not good, I tell myself sternly. Stick to the facts. Emotions cloud judgement. I know this well. But I'm beginning to suspect it may be too late.

Despite my mixed feelings about selling the house, I still contact a colleague of Amir's who he recommends I reach out to. She's a fellow real estate agent who specializes in high value homes. As a favor because I'm a friend of Amir's, she compiles some sales figures for comparable houses that have sold in the surrounding area in the last few years. There aren't many, but she is able to give me a ballpark amount of a fair asking price. It's higher than I thought, which is good news, and I'm glad to have a figure in mind in case Amir's clients do want to make an offer.

I sleep late Saturday morning and then slip out for a long run before I even have a cup of tea. I just need to clear my head. When I get back an hour later, there's a plumber's truck parked in front of the house. The front doors are open wide and the dogs are running in and out, barking wildly.

"Oh that doesn't look good," I frown. I sprint into the house. In the front entrance hall, Poppy is conferring with a heavyset man holding a wrench who I assume is the plumber.

"A pipe burst in the dining room ceiling," she tells me, rolling her eyes. "It's a complete mess."

Just then Cameron strides in from the direction of the

kitchen. I've never seen him look anything but cool and calm, but now there's a definite edge to him and two spots of color are burning high on those sharp cheekbones.

"I dinnae have any water in the kitchen!" he exclaims.

Poppy explains the situation and Cameron shoots her an alarmed glance. "We've got a full house tonight for the supper club," he says, then turns to the plumber. "How long did you say the water will be off?"

The man shrugs and hitches up his pants. "Dunno, mate. Hours at the least. Might be overnight. It's a tricky repair. We're going to have to take up the tile in the upstairs bathroom."

"And how am I supposed to cook for guests with no running water?" Cameron demands.

Poppy chews her lip and grimaces. "Maybe cancel the evening and postpone a week?"

Cameron groans and utters a very Scottish oath. "Any other week I would, but I canna cancel tonight. There's a restaurant critic from The Herald who's coming all the way from Glasgow. She's featuring us in an article on the rise of supper clubs. The article is supposed to run on Monday. If we cancel tonight, we lose the newspaper exposure and she loses her story. We canna cancel on her now. " He looks exasperated.

The plumber frowns. "Bad luck, aye mate? We're going as fast as we can, but I canna make any promises."

Cameron nods wearily. "Aye," he says. "Thanks all the same." He puts his hands on his hips and stares out the door, thinking. "And Kenny just called. He got himself scraped up in a cycling accident on the way over just now. Hit a cow in the road, dinnae ask me how. He's sprained his wrist and canna lift anything for a week so he's not coming in today." He drums his fingers on his hips and frowns, trying to figure a way out of this mess.

"I'll help." The words are out of my mouth before I even realize it.

He turns to me, seeming to register for the first time that I'm standing here. "Avery," he looks surprised to see me. "What did you say?"

"I'll help," I offer. "I'm not a trained chef, but I know my way around a kitchen."

"I can help, too," Poppy says. "Freddie can keep an eye on the kids and Avery and I can be your servers and sous-chefs. Louise will be there too, right?"

Cameron considers our offer for a moment, then nods slowly. "It's possible it could still work. I'll have to simplify the menu," he muses.

"And I think we're going to have to serve the meal in the garden because the dining room is a mess of wet plaster," Poppy adds with a grimace. "But the weather is nice."

Cameron narrows his eyes, thinking. "Aye, maybe we can pull this off, if we're lucky." He heaves a sigh, then looks at both of us and seems to reach a decision. "Let's give it a go then," he says. "Come on, we've got a lot to do before the guests arrive."

He's already striding back down the hall toward the kitchen, calling instructions to us over his shoulder. Poppy peels off to text Freddie and fill him in on our plan. I follow Cameron into the kitchen. It's Saturday, and I was planning to rustle up some cheese from the kitchen and curl up in the library with a romance between a highwayman with a heart of gold and a runaway duchess, but I hastily abandon that plan. This is more important, and honestly more interesting. Cameron tosses me an apron and I slip it on and tie it around my waist. He's moving around the kitchen, talking to himself and rapidly opening drawers, rattling silverware and pulling things from the pantry.

"A three-course meal with a garden party theme," he

mutters to himself. He turns to me. "Let's see what we can do in the garden."

I follow him outside where we brainstorm about how to transform a badly neglected formal garden into an elegant garden party venue in a matter of hours.

"We dinnae have time to trim the hedges and tidy everything," Cameron says with a sigh.

"Maybe we do a sort of Midsummer Nights Dream kind of theme," I suggest. "Embrace the unkemptness and make it look magical."

"Magical," Cameron looks doubtful. "If you and Poppy can make this overgrown mess look magical, you'll have my undying gratitude. Can you handle setting it up for fourteen guests? They start arriving at five."

I gulp and check my phone. Can we transform this space and have dinner ready in a little less than five hours? Without running water?

"We've got this," I tell him more confidently than I feel. "You worry about dinner. Let us handle the ambience." Then I hurry to find Poppy.

Chapter 14

"You've worked a blessed miracle," Cameron says when he sees what we've managed to do. I have to agree. It's taken us almost three hours, but Poppy and I have worked a miracle. With Freddie's help, we hauled two heavy old tables out into the garden and Poppy found two nice tablecloths tucked away in a linen closet and hastily ironed them. The twins and I scavenged a small copse of woods behind the manor house and by a stroke of luck found a few patches of bluebells which we picked and put in small vases and jars down the center of the table, nestled between long fronds of bracken. We found candles and put them in charmingly mismatched glass jars, then strung up two strands of fairy lights above the tables, and gathered every cozy blanket and knitted afghan around the manor for the guests as it will get chilly when evening falls. The twins really got into the spirit of things and proved to be tireless and motivated little workers. I even managed to locate a pair of hedge clippers in the detached garage behind the house, and we allowed an enthusiastic Grant to trim the most egregious of the hedges into a slightly more respectable shape. The result of all our efforts, when we step back, is truly magical. The tables are set with fine china and crystal, and with the floral arrangements, candles, and the background of the sea, the effect is one of faded grandeur and a whimsical, fairy-like beauty.

"Oh it's amazing," Poppy breathes in delight, clapping her hands. Cameron raises an eyebrow. "I suppose that'll do," he says gruffly, but I can tell he's feeling relieved and pleased. "No rest for the wicked," he tells us with a wink at the twins. "Avery, I need your hands in the kitchen if you're done out here."

I use a precious cup of water from a pitcher by the sink in the kitchen to scrub my hands as best I can, and then present myself to Cameron. "Reporting for duty."

He appears to be assembling salmon and goat cheese appetizers. Thankfully the bread and cheese were already made. Louise is in the kitchen with him, clad in an apron that is too big for her, elbow deep in sliced cucumbers. Freddie appears from the cellar, arms filled with bottles of wine. He's going to keep an eye on the children and act as sommelier for the evening.

"How are you at whipping cream?" Cameron asks me, pausing over his tray of appetizers.

"A question literally no one has ever asked me," I tell him, then add, "I can manage to whip cream, I'm sure."

"Good," He pulls a cold mixing bowl from the freezer and a container of cream from the refrigerator. "Have you ever made cranachan?"

"Um, no. I've had it once or twice though."

It's a classic Scottish dessert – a trifle of sorts - made by layering toasted oats softened in whipping cream with fresh raspberries flavored with honey and whisky. Cameron pulls out a skillet and dumps some raw oats into the pan, puts it on the Aga and hands me a wooden spoon. "They should be toasted, not burnt," he commands briskly in that delicious burr. "Watch them carefully, aye?"

I stir the oats but instead of watching the pan, I watch him stride around the kitchen rearranging the menu, giving orders to Louise and Poppy when she comes in, and keeping one eye on me.

"Dinnae forget to stir!" he commands from the other side of the room without even looking at me. He's slicing lemons with speed and precision. I have to admit, watching him cook is impressive. He's fully in command of this kitchen, like a general mustering troops.

How long has it been since I was part of a team? Years at least. I'm always the one in charge, always the one swooping in to fix something. I work solo most of the time, or with strangers. It's novel to be part of a team I know for a change, to be taking orders from a bearded clansman ruling his kitchen kingdom with authority. I glance down in time to see a large hand close over mine.

"Concentrate," he commands in a murmur, his breath warm against the shell of my ear. I can feel him behind me, a solid wall of muscle pressed for a moment against my back. I shiver, then do as I'm told and stir.

We work with brisk efficiency. Cameron roasts three chickens and finishes the appetizer platters while I assemble the cranachan. Poppy whips the herbed butter and puts the rolls in baskets. Louise helps out wherever she's needed. We listen to loud music – The Rolling Stones, The Cure, Led Zeppelin. I mash a bowl full of ripe red raspberries to "Just Like Heaven" and whip whisky and honey into the cream while Mick Jagger wails about not always getting what we want. With twenty minutes until the guests arrive, I finish all of my assigned tasks and go to Cameron for my next orders. He's standing in the garden, surveying everything with an assessing look.

"Everything look okay?" I ask, coming to stand beside him.

My pulse is starting to slow now after so many hours fueled by adrenaline.

He looks around. "Aye, everything is bonny, thanks to you and Poppy." He clears his throat and slants me a questioning look. "Why did you offer help?" he asks. "I ken you're not the biggest fan of my restaurant idea."

I consider the question. So many possible answers I could give. Because I want to be near him which is, I am aware, one of my less noble motivations. Because I want to see firsthand how he does under pressure and how he runs his kitchen. This answer makes sense from a business perspective. But really the truth is much simpler.

"Because you needed the help," I tell him honestly, gazing up at him. He scrubs a hand down his face and says a swear word, low and hoarse.

"Avery," he looks at me with an expression that almost looks pained. He seems at a loss for words.

"What?" I'm alarmed by that look. I can't decipher it.

"Nothing," he mutters. "Come on then. The guests will be arriving soon." His fingers close around my arm, warm and strong as he guides me back to the kitchen. I have just enough time to run up to my room to change into something a little more festive, slick on some lipstick and run a brush through my hair. Poppy knocks on my door to give me the happy news that the plumbers are done and that we have running water again. Perfect timing as I hear the crunch of tires on gravel outside just as I'm coming down the stairs. We pour flutes of champagne and stand by the open doors to welcome the firsts guests as they arrive. I breathe a sigh of relief. Somehow we've managed to pull this off by the skin of our teeth.

The rest of the evening passes in a blur of happy chatter, soft music, the clink of wine glasses, and laughter drifting on the breeze. The guests seem delighted by the adventure of a magical al fresco dinner by the sea. Even the restaurant reviewer, an energetic sprite of a woman with curly red hair and an impish sense of humor, seems charmed by... everything. The wine, the food, the ambience, and especially Cameron. She flirts with him every chance she gets.

The dinner is delicious. Smoked salmon and herbed goat cheese on homemade oat cakes for a starter followed by pork hand pies, the crusts flaky from lard and the filling savory with meat and herbs from the manor house garden. Three roast chickens and rolls with fresh butter accompanied by new potatoes, a cucumber salad, and honey glazed roasted carrots for the main course. Poppy, Louise, and I help serve and Freddie keeps the wine flowing. The twins are upstairs, rewarded for their good behavior with a Disney movie and ice cream. The evening is going well, and I find myself energized and buoyed by getting to be a part of it. Just like when I helped make the cheese, I find I'm having fun.

I'm whisking away the main course plates when Poppy comes up to me, hovering at my elbow. "He watches you, you know," she says conspiratorially, leaning in close and nodding toward Cameron. We both glance at him as he describes the process of harvesting the honey to the dinner guests who are listening with rapt attention, particularly the red-haired restaurant critic. Poppy is right. Cameron keeps glancing at me while he talks to the guests. Our eyes snag, and for a moment he doesn't look away. I break the connection, looking down at the dirty plates in my hands, feeling suddenly off-kilter.

Poppy sighs. "Most women would kill for a good man to look at them like that, big sis. Especially one with those calves." She tosses me a wink, nods toward the fine calves in question, and heads toward the far end of the table to gather more dishes. Spooked, I grab the dirty dishes nearest me and hightail it to the kitchen.

At the sink I turn and stare out the window into the gardens. Soon it will be time to serve the dessert I made. I'm inordinately proud of how the cranachan turned out. It's a simple dish, but I made it myself, and that feels special. Currently it's sitting prettily in the refrigerator, rows of trifle glasses with alternating layers of raspberries, oats, and cream. I catch sight of Cameron standing next to a guest at the table and my heart thumps heavily. He's talking to the restaurant critic who is laughing up at him. She's asking him questions and gesturing to the various components of the meal. She touches his arm flirtatiously and he steps back a little, his eyes flitting to the window where I am watching. I back away as though scalded, and lean against the sink, heart thumping. Why are his eyes tracking me like that? Why am I noticing?

"Keep it together, Avery," I warn, but I know it's too late. For the second time in my life, I'm falling for Cameron MacKay.

* * *

Hours later the dinner party is over. It was, by all accounts, a rousing success. The guests have departed happy and well fed. Freddie and Poppy are upstairs putting the twins to bed and Cameron sent Louise back to their cottage to take a well-earned break. Now all that remains are the last few dishes and a few small tasks to close out the night. Cameron is outside snuffing out the candles and bringing in the last of the dishes. I'm standing at the sink, hands in soapy water, ostensibly washing crystal wine glasses. What I'm actually doing is watching Cameron. He gathers the final few items on the table and heads inside. I look up when he comes in, then quickly away, concentrating on a wine glass with a bright red lipstick mark on the rim. A moment later I feel a big hand close around my elbow.

"Avery, is something amiss?" His tone is concerned. I shake my head, scrubbing at the stain firmly and not looking at him. If I do, I'm afraid of what I'll see on his face. I'm afraid of what he may see in mine. This can't happen. Attraction, a crush, desire, whatever this is, it isn't professional, and I have to keep things professional. It's safer to keep things professional.

"I'm great," I say in a tone of forced cheer. "What a night, huh?" But he doesn't fall for the ploy.

"Och, Avery, will you look at me?" he gently turns me to face him and tilts my chin up. I meet his eyes reluctantly, feeling my face flame. My hands are dripping soapy water on the floor. He searches my eyes, his own questioning. "What's wrong?" he asks. Without looking he takes a towel from the counter and hands it to me.

"Nothing," I insist, moving away and drying my hands on the towel. I'm lying. We both know it. "It was a really fun night."

"Have I done something to upset you?" he asks, sounding genuinely concerned. "You havena looked in my direction all night."

Not true. I feel like all I've done all night is track his whereabouts. Apparently now I have developed excellent Cameron radar, I know where he is at all times.

"What's amiss, lass?" he asks softly, refusing to let it go.

"Nothing's amiss," I insist. I think of the impending arrival of Amir and the California couple tomorrow and push the reminder away. I'll worry about them later.

He waits patiently, his silence pressing me for the truth. "I just...I just...this is too much." I blurt out. What I mean is, *I like you too much*, but I refuse to say the words. You can't take them back once they're said.

He looks puzzled. "What's too much?"

"Everything," I burst out, moving away from him so the

island is between us. I need space to breathe, to keep my distance which is becoming increasingly difficult with this man. "Family dinners. Monopoly by the fire even if Maeve beats me every time and I can never land on Mayfair or Park Lane. Everything you cook is delicious. I'm going to waddle home in stretchy pants. You. This life. Getting to be part of a team. It's just... it's just..."

"Just what?" he crosses his arms and watches me patiently. I have the feeling he will wait all night.

"It scares me," I admit finally in a small voice. "I work alone. I don't let things get permanent or messy or complicated, ever. I do my job, a damn good job, and then I move on. I like things neat, tidy, and compartmentalized. Not like..." I gesture around me, "this."

Cameron arches a brow, his expression bordering on amusement. "That sounds boring," he says finally. Boring? I open my mouth to protest but shut it with a snap. He's not wrong.

"It is boring," I admit finally. "But it's mine and it's safe. That's the way I like it. No risk."

Cameron shakes his head slowly. "Liar," he says calmly. I gape at him.

"What? How can you say that? You know nothing about my life," I insist with an indignant scowl.

"I ken you well, Avery," he says reasonably, slowly moving around the island, closing the distance between us. "I never told you this, but I had such a big crush on you when we were in high school. You were so smart, so competitive, so bonny, and so damn determined. I used to hope you'd come into the chippy every time I had a shift, and when you did, I dinnae ever want you to leave. You were a mystery, utterly fascinating to me. And then I watched you after Ellen died, how scared and grieved you were when you came back to Oban, but so determined to succeed. You are the most bloody stubborn woman I have ever met. You're so capable you could probably run the world, but you're a coward when it comes to your own heart."

I stand there open mouthed as the revelations keep coming and he keeps moving closer, as relaxed and purposeful as a cat. I get the unnerving feeling that I'm being backed into a corner, even though I'm not moving.

"You dinnae really want a sterile, empty life, Avery," Cameron says firmly. "You want something more, but what you want scares you because there's risk involved, aye, and you're afraid to lose anything else you care about." He stops a few feet away, giving me space. I take a gasping little breath.

"It makes sense, ye ken," he continues softly. "That you've shut your life into a lonely little box because you think it's safe. But that's not what makes you happy, that's not what you really want."

"Oh really?" I say coolly while my pulse is racing. I feel so caught out and exposed it takes every ounce of effort not to flee. I want to cozy up in my Slanket and eat an entire wedge of Wensleydale with apricots right this instant. I want to hop a plane to Chicago and jump back into my old life. Dismantling a sports bar in Wisconsin sounds safe and easy right about now. How fast can I pack?

"How do you know what I want?" I demand, lifting my chin defiantly.

He takes it as an invitation. He moves faster than a big man should be able to. In an instant he's wrapping me in his arms, pressing me between his body and the granite of the island. I feel every inch of him, the hard muscles of his abdomen, his big hands splayed across my back, the scratchy wool of his kilt brushing against my fingers.

"Because I think you want me like I want you," he whispers in my ear. And then he kisses me. It's a surprisingly gentle kiss, a brush of lips, almost tender. He pauses, giving me a moment to refuse. To my consternation, I do exactly the opposite. Almost without thinking I stand on my tiptoes, grab the back of his neck and press my mouth to his eagerly. A little embarrassing whimper of need escapes me and when he hears it he growls low in his throat and instantly steps between my thighs. He tastes of sage and lemon thyme and a touch of honey sweetness and a hint of whisky. One taste and I can't get enough. I whimper again, a demand. He responds to me. One hand comes up and cups the back of my head as he slants his mouth across mine, so hungry yet I feel as though he is restraining himself, as though he wants to devour me. I bite his full lower lip and feel him jerk in surprise, then he gives in and takes my mouth roughly, deliciously. The world tilts and I feel myself sway, suddenly dizzy, but he's got me, holding me up. I've never felt safer or more out of control. I make a little noise in my throat, trying to wiggle closer to him, and suddenly he releases me and backs away so swiftly that I almost crumple. I grab the edge of the island to steady myself. My legs are like jelly. We stare at each other, dumbfounded, breathing heavily. I've never been kissed like that in my life. I want more. I want all of it.

"No," he says finally, almost harshly. "This is not the way we're going to do this."

"Do what?" I pant.

"Whatever this is between us," he says, gesturing to the space between his body and mine. "You must choose for yourself what you want, Avery. I'll not sway you with kisses and promises. I make no promises, hear? I want you. That should be bloody obvious, but this is your choice alone. You have to take the risk yourself for the life you want. I willna do it for you, lass." He stares at me, looking almost angry, and then he wheels around and leaves abruptly.

I feel suddenly cold, bereft of the warm weight of him anchoring me. For those few brief moments, it felt like heaven to be held, wanted and warmed. Shaken, I press my fingers to my lips. I can still taste him. I'm lightheaded with need.

"I don't know what I want," I whisper to the empty kitchen, but even as I voice the words, I know they're a lie. I want two contradictory things. To be loved and a part of something bigger than me. And to keep myself safe by holding back, being cautious and canny, avoiding risk. That way I can't lose something precious if I only rely on myself. I can't fail and others can't fail me.

Cameron is right. Two paths lie before me – keep myself safe and go my own way, or risk everything and stay. These are conflicting desires; I understand I cannot have both. I am going to have to choose, and soon.

Chapter 15

"These Scottish roads are madness but the vistas are superb!" Amir announces as he alights from the hired sedan late the next morning, looking crisp and well-turned out in a beige linen suit and perfectly polished Italian leather loafers. We embrace in the driveway and he whispers in my ear.

"They liked the chateau, so you're going to have to really sell them on the manor." Then he air kisses my cheek and says loudly. "Darling, what a pleasure. Thank you for letting us have this exclusive sneak peek at such a highly sought after property." He winks at me slyly and turns solicitously to usher his companions from the car.

The couple who get out of the back seat are in their fifties – the man florid, well-fed, with a golf shirt unbuttoned at the collar and greying hair swept back from his receding hairline. He looks around him with the air of a man used to getting exactly what he wants. He sees me and sticks out his hand, handshake firm. I meet it and hold his eyes for a second, letting him know I'm not a lackey who will scrape and bow.

"Ed Butler," he says shortly. "Nice place you have here. Helluva drive on those roads though."

I laugh lightly. "They can be a challenge until you get used to them, but you look like a man who enjoys a good challenge."

He grunts in reply but eyes me with a smidge more respect. I turn smoothly to his wife who has alighted behind him and is looking around her in wide-eyed wonder. She's tiny, with champagne blonde hair pulled back with a headband, dressed like she's going to play tennis. Everything is tasteful and understated which screams money. When I take her hand, it feels like clutching the claw of a finch or a sparrow.

"Evelyn Butler," she says a little breathlessly, looking up at the front of the house looming above us. "Oh," her lips part. "Ed, it... it reminds me of Lallybroch, but even bigger and more grand."

Ed pauses his conversation with Amir and glances at his wife. For an instant his face softens, then he frowns. "Better be a lot more modern than that show you like to watch," he growls. "I'm not paying top dollar for bad plumbing."

My stomach, already in knots, loops itself into another figure eight. The plumbing on these old houses is notoriously unreliable. The house has modern conveniences, barely. Out of the corner of my eye, I see Poppy and Freddie come out the kitchen door and head for the Landcruiser, the twins in tow. They're on their way to church this morning, so the timing is perfect. Poppy gives a little wave and I wave back surreptitiously. I told them that a friend of mine was in the area with some of his clients, touring old houses, and that I'd offered to give them a quick tour of our house. I did not mention why they were touring old houses. I don't want to get too far ahead of myself and cause any unnecessary drama. I don't even know if they're interested in the house. If they are... well, then I'll be forced to make a decision.

The day is lovely, partly sunny with a fresh breeze off the bay. I show them around the grounds, emphasizing the history of the house and telling a few personal anecdotes from our family lore, like the time our great-uncle Aaron rode through the formal garden backwards on a donkey on a dare and was dumped into the fountain by the cantankerous beast. Evelyn seems charmed by everything. She rhapsodizes about the Scottish baronial architecture and oohs and aahs over the sweeping sea views. Ed is a harder nut to crack. He is a businessman to the core, unswayed by sentimentality. He wants to know acreage (a lot), property taxes (moderate), and cost of upkeep (high). He chews gum and takes everything in with a keen, observant eye. But he seems to have a soft spot for his wife, and she seems to have a soft spot for Scotland.

"Tell them about the village," Amir urges under his breath, and I describe the quaint town of Oban. "It's the seafood capital of Scotland," I say proudly. "And a wonderful, warm, and charming community."

We head inside through the big front doors. I show them the bedrooms and bathrooms, sitting rooms and even the now-unused servant's quarters in the attic. Evelyn loves the faded cabbage rose wallpaper on the walls in the bigger front parlor, the worn velvet love seats, and pretty little writing desks. She is enamored with the upstairs picture gallery, its rows of generations of stern-faced Hayes ancestors looking down their long noses in disapproval.

I feel guilty somehow, showing them the house, although I am completely within my rights to do so. I keep thinking of last night, of that fervent kiss, of Cameron breaking away so as not to sway my decision. Too late. I am swayed. I don't want to admit it, but last night swayed me. I've been subtly swayed since I arrived, not just by Cameron, by all of it. Not enough to make a rash decision, but enough to make me uncomfortable with my own ambivalence.

This is not a decision to be made from sentimentality or because of a crush. I need to be clear headed and strategic. The delicious divot at the dip of Cameron's upper lip does not factor in. At least it shouldn't. I shake myself and try to concentrate on selling the charms of this old house.

We see the kitchen last, and as I lead them through the stone passageway, I'm hoping it will be empty. Unfortunately it isn't. Cameron and Kenny are both there, wearing aprons and hard at work. From the look and aroma of things, they're making some sort of chutney. Perfect. I sigh inwardly. Cameron looks up, startled at our appearance. He's dicing apples and there are piles of raisins and chopped onions in bowls next to him. Kenny is at the stove stirring something tangy and spicy with cinnamon and vinegar.

"Good morning," Cameron says warily, his eyes flicking to me and then to Amir and the Butlers.

"Oh," squeaks Evelyn. I look over at her. The tip of her nose has gone pink from excitement.

"Allow me to introduce Cameron MacKay, a celebrated local chef who uses our kitchen from time to time," I say cheerfully. "Looks like we caught him on chutney day."

Cameron gives me a bemused look as he takes a spoon and tastes whatever Kenny is stirring. "Aye," he says. "Today it's an apple spice chutney with apples from our own orchard here on the manor grounds."

Evelyn presses her hand to her chest and fawns over every word. Ed shoots her an annoyed glance. "Don't get too attached," he says gruffly. "I'm sure the man does not come with the property."

At those words, Cameron's head whips up and he shoots me a narrow glance. I pretend not to see. "Let's take a quick peek in the pantry and then I've prepared a special little Scottish tea time for you. We can take it out to the garden while I answer any questions you may have."

While they poke their heads in the pantry, I pull out a plate of scones I purchased at the store in anticipation of their arrival and put the kettle on the Aga.

"I don't come with the property?" Cameron says in a low voice as I pass by him with the scones. "Avery, who are these people? What's going on?" I can feel his eyes on me, demanding answers.

I don't look at him. "Amir is an old friend and he had clients who were interested in seeing the house. Nothing's decided." But I feel a little guilty all the same, and annoyed for feeling guilty. I made it clear that if Cameron's idea didn't knock my socks off, I was selling the house. It is my choice. Poppy and I agreed. But telling myself that doesn't make it feel better.

"They want to buy the house," he says flatly, setting down his knife and looking at me. I feel instantly defensive, but take a deep breath and answer calmly.

"Nothing is settled. It's just good business sense to know your options."

He makes a very Scottish sounding snort of disapproval in his throat and goes back to chopping apples, shaking his head and muttering darkly, too low for me to make out the words. I'm sure they're not complimentary. I tell myself I don't care.

Ten minutes later I have the Butlers situated at a small outdoor table enjoying tea time with scones and jam, some shortbread fingers, and of course a good Scottish breakfast tea. From the look of it, both are having a good time. Ed is on his third shortbread finger already and Evelyn hasn't stopped rhapsodizing long enough to take a sip of her tea.

"How do you think it's going?" I pull Amir aside, near a leggy climbing rose bush that is bending over a stone bench. I brought a cup of tea and a shortbread finger for him. He hands the shortbread back to me promptly.

"Oh sweetie, I haven't eaten carbs since 2019," he tells me confidently, brushing aside a long rose cane that is dangling near his ear. We really need to get this garden under control.

"What do you think? Do they like it more than the chateau?" I ask, glancing over at the Butlers. Evelyn is still talking and Ed is now tucking into the scones.

"She seems very taken with it," Amir admits. "But we will have to see about Ed. He had his heart set on something warmer. Scotland is dreary for his taste, but he has a soft spot for Evelyn. They have four grown children and are wanting a place where the family can gather for holidays and vacations. If she wants this place, my guess is they'll make an offer on it. We will just have to wait and see."

I glance over at the Butlers, trying to imagine giving them the keys, clearing out all our personal belongings, relinquishing ownership of our ancestral family home. It gives me a pang in my heart.

"And we could have Christmas here, and summer holidays," I overhear Evelyn saying. "Did you hear her say there's lots of fishing? You've always wanted to take up fishing, Ed. And there's so much room in the house, too. Everyone could have their own bedroom, even the grandbabies. Can't you just see Alicia and Jon and the twins here? Oh Ed, it would be such a good place for our family. Just think of it."

She looks up at the house with shining eyes. I should feel relieved and grateful. I did what I set out to do. I've found a buyer for Haye House. So why do I not feel more celebratory? I stuff the thought away. I will be plenty happy and relieved when we're not saddled with this money pit of a house. I think of my half of the sale price and try to picture the cottage on

Bainbridge Island. Every day will be a Saturday, I remind myself.

Before, the thought has always warmed my heart, but today I feel only a dull sort of resignation. What is wrong with me? I give myself a mental shake and go join the Butlers to answer any questions they may have. When they depart thirty minutes later, Evelyn waving enthusiastically from the open sedan window, all their questions have been answered, but I realize mine have only gotten louder.

Chapter 16

The knock on my bedroom door late Sunday night surprises me.

"Just a minute!" I rub my grainy eyes and get up from the writing desk in the corner of my room. It's covered in charts, graphs, and financial documents that I've been pouring over since Amir left with the Butlers. He called an hour after they drove away to say the Butlers want to make an offer on the house and he would be drawing up the paperwork tomorrow. The number they are planning to offer is very generous. Since the call, I've been going back and forth in my head about my decision, pouring over my spreadsheets, checking my figures. On paper it's clear what the prudent decision is. Sell the house.

"I'm coming," I call again, shutting my laptop and hoping it's Poppy and not Cameron. I've been hiding up here, trying to avoid Cameron. After our passionate embrace last night and his reaction today in the kitchen to seeing Amir and the Butlers, I am not eager to run into him until I've made my decision.

I open the door.

"Louise?" She's literally the last person on the property I expected to be standing there.

"Sorry ta bother ye so late," she murmurs, hovering just outside the doorway in the dark hallway. She's wearing a pair of Smurf pajamas and twisting the string of the pajama pants nervously.

"Do you need something?" I ask cautiously. I don't want to spook her. I have the feeling that she's half a second away from bolting down the hall.

"I..." she glances behind her down the empty corridor. Then she turns to me and catches her bottom lip between her teeth, worrying it. She seems to be summoning her courage. She looks up at me, takes a deep breath, and asks. "Could I talk to ye?"

"Oh, sure. Of course. How about a cup of tea?"

She nods and I join her in the hallway, shutting my door behind me. "Does your dad know you're here?"

She hesitates, then shakes her head. "That's why I want to talk to ye," she says. "It's about him."

Puzzled and intrigued, I motion for her to follow and head barefoot to the kitchen. Maybe a cup of tea and some shortbread will ease the awkwardness and help her say whatever she's come to say. I lead the way through the house in my favorite Stanford hoodie from freshman year and a pair of tiny cotton shorts. It's chilly in the hallway and I wish I'd thought to wear longer pants or at least find my slippers. Too late now.

The kitchen is cozy and warm with the constant steady heat of the Aga, and I sigh with relief. I switch the lights on and blink in the sudden glare. The overhead lights buzz as they flicker to life. It smells like the apple chutney Cameron was making earlier – warm and tangy and rich with spices - and my stomach growls. I was so tied up in my calculations and deliberations after the Butler's visit that I skipped dinner entirely.

It's late, past ten p.m., and now I'm famished. I put the kettle on and head to the pantry. The dogs are curled up by the Aga, snoozing. In the pantry I find a packet of shortbread fingers and a few scones left over from the Butler's tea party. Back at the kitchen island I shake a few shortbread fingers onto a plate and pile on a few scones, too. I munch on a shortbread finger. Louise is crouching by the dog bed, scratching a sleepy but delighted Daisy behind the ears. Daisy rolls onto her back and stretches.

"So what can I help you with?" I ask conversationally. Louise straightens and hesitates for a minute. Then she looks me straight in the eye.

"Please dinnae sell the house to the Americans," she blurts out.

"Ah." So she knows about the Butlers. I heave a sigh.

"I heard my dad talking to Uncle Freddie about it," she explains, coming over to the island. She glances at me, her expression unsure. "He said you might be plannin' to sell it to them."

Oh boy, if Freddie knows about the Butler's visit, it's only a matter of time until Poppy finds out. I wonder how long it will take her to track me down and try to sway my decision. She can be mighty persuasive when she sets her mind to something. I don't relish the thought of that conversation.

"Nothing is decided," I assure Louise "But tell me, why do you think I shouldn't sell the house to the Butlers?" I snag a scone and slide the plate over to her. Louise frowns, thinking. She takes a scone but doesn't eat it, just crumbles it between her fingers nervously.

"If you sell, then all our hard work here willna matter. Dad has worked hard to build a home for us and to put food on the table, and to turn this place into his dream, ye ken," she says slowly. "If you sell, he'll have to get a job in a restaurant in town. He's a braw chef, but it's not what he wants, to work for someone else." She pauses. "And I heard him say to Uncle

Freddie that there isna another property that would work half as well any closer than Fort William.

"And you don't want to move to Fort William?" I guess.

She shakes her head, looking down and picking at the crumbled bits of her scone. "I... moved a lot when I was younger," she admits quietly. "This is the longest I've ever lived anywhere. I dinnae want to leave. It's a bonnie place." She darts a cautious glance at me.

I lean my hip against the counter and study her, trying to imagine growing up in her environment - the instability, being shuffled from place to place. My parents were emotionally absent, but at least they provided a stable home for us. We lived in the same brick Colonial for my entire childhood. And even when they were off doing their research, they left us in good hands. In a way, their absence gave us the biggest touchstones of our lives, Aunt Ellen and this house. I cannot imagine a world in which I had not had either. Yet that was Louise's reality up until Cameron came for her.

Daisy gets up with a soft whoof and comes over to Louise. The dog noses her, as if to comfort her, then leans her bulk against Louise's leg. Louise scratches her blocky head and smiles. The dogs clearly adore her, and vice versa. I remember Maeve commenting that Louise knows everything about animals. I read somewhere that when children have experienced trauma, often it's easier for them to connect with animals than with people. I think of the goats and baby Highland cows outside in the stable, of the chickens and bees. I wonder how much courage it took for Louise to come approach me. She must want to stay very badly.

"What do you want me to do?" I ask her softly.

Louise looks up quickly, her green eyes lit with a sudden spark of hope. "Give Dad a chance to try his idea before you sell the house," she asks quietly. "Please?"

"It took courage for you to approach me, Louise," I tell her. "And I respect that. So I'm going to level with you. It doesn't make sense for me not to sell this place. I have a buyer who's making a good offer. I never wanted to keep this house, and selling it is the best move for me financially."

It's more than that, I know. It's the safest move emotionally, too. Unbidden, I think of making the burrata with Cameron, the feel of the smooth mozzarella between my fingers, the feel of his hand guiding mine. Maybe I don't want to just eat cheese anymore, I think suddenly. Maybe I want to make it, too. I push the thought aside.

"I haven't decided anything," I tell Louise finally.

"What have you not decided?" Poppy pops into the kitchen from the darkened hall like a rabbit from its burrow. She's wearing a robe over pajama pants and a lace trimmed tank top, and her hair is a wild bramble of red curls.

I give a little yelp of surprise at her sudden appearance. "I haven't decided if I'm going to sell the house," I tell her. "Louise is asking me not to."

Poppy narrows her eyes at me suspiciously. "I heard those people who saw the house today weren't just touring old houses. Freddie told me they're potential buyers?" She stares me down. I lift my chin and return the stare.

"They're making us a generous offer on the house tomorrow," I confirm.

"What about our agreement?" Poppy protests. "You said you'd give Cam a fair shake."

"And I have," I argue. "But any way I slice it, it's a risk. Cameron's business proposal is a great idea, but the prudent choice is to sell while we have a good offer."

Poppy comes to stand by Louise at the island. She spies the plate of treats.

"Ooh, a warm scone wouldn't go amiss." She picks one up,

cuts it in half with a butter knife, and puts it in the toaster. Then she turns and stares at me. "But you're not convinced you want to sell, are you?" she asks shrewdly.

I hesitate, then shake my head. "I'm stuck," I admit. "I don't know what the right thing is to do." My head and my heart are at odds.

"Why don't you read your tea leaves?" Poppy asks, rolling her eyes at me. "Why have a gift if you don't even use it?"

I have not considered that idea, in fact. I hesitate. It's been so long. Will I even remember what to do? I think of Aunt Ellen. I imagine she's been heartbroken that I'd given it up for so long. Now I'm here again, in Oban, and needing advice. What could be the harm? Maybe it will give me a nudge in the right direction.

Louise is looking between us, intrigued. "Are you a reader then?" she asks, eyes wide with curiosity.

"She is," Poppy confirms. "A very good one, too. Though a bit out of practice now." She looks at me reprimandingly.

"Okay," I agree. "Let's read the tea leaves."

Chapter 17

Poppy gives a little shriek of excitement at my agreement and runs into the pantry, coming back with a dusty old-fashioned glass jar. I recognize it instantly. "No one's used this since you left," she announces. "Since you're the only one in the family who can read leaves now."

"Maybe Maeve will have the gift. You never know," I tell her, taking the jar carefully. How many times did I see Aunt Ellen grab this jar and disappear into the back room with someone from the village who came to her seeking advice and guidance? More times than I can count. And here we are again, seeking the same guidance.

"I think your scone is scorching," Louise says, pointing to the toaster with concern. A thin plume of smoke is drifting lazily from the top.

"Oh jinks!" Poppy flicks up the lever and snatches the two blackened halves of her scone from the toaster, chucking them in the rubbish bin with a grimace. "We really have to get a new one of those some day," she frowns at the toaster. "Always something going wrong around this place." With a sigh she goes to check the water in the kettle on the Aga, swiping a shortbread finger on her way.

"Can you read my leaves, too?" she asks casually, lifting the lid of the kettle.

"Sure," I agree. "Do you want me to read your tea leaves?" I offer Louise.

She hesitates, then nods shyly. "Aye, that'd be braw. I've never seen it done before," she admits. "How does it work?"

"The patterns the leaves make in the bottom of the cup give us a little peek into the future," I explain while I measure out the loose leaf tea into three shallow white teacups I grab from the cupboard. "It's a tradition in Scotland, to consult the tea leaves when you need some direction. Some people think it's just superstition, but others find it helps them make good decisions. My Aunt Ellen was the most celebrated tea reader in all of the West Highlands. She trained me to carry on the tradition."

"She tried to train me, but I was a failure," Poppy announces cheerfully from the stove. "I don't have the gift like Avery. You have to have the gift for it to work. Water's hot."

Poppy brings the kettle over and fills the cups with hot water. I stir the loose leaf tea, the familiar aroma drifting lazily up in a waft of steam. The tea is Aunt Ellen's special blend, a combination of Scottish breakfast tea, thistle, and heather. Aunt Ellen swore that the mixture produced the most clear and accurate readings. This tea blend is a good ten years old, but it should still work fine. I inhale the faint earthy, bitter scent, reminded of so many summers sitting next to Aunt Ellen doing exactly this. It makes me miss her.

"Now we let it steep."

We eat shortbread cookies while we stand around the island

in silence. For three minutes the only sounds in the kitchen are the ticking of the clock and the crunch of buttery shortbread fingers.

"Okay, time's up," I announce. It's been three minutes. The tea leaves have all settled to the bottom of the cups and the tea is a clear reddish brown. "Drink the tea slowly and carefully. Don't disturb the leaves," I instruct. "And while you drink it, think about the question you want to ask," I hand cups to Poppy and Louise. "Concentrate on a single question you're seeking an answer to."

I drink my tea slowly, the warmth trickling down my throat and into my belly where I feel a little tickle of nerves. It's been years since I read leaves. The last time was with Aunt Ellen. Now here I am, on my own, hoping for clarity. Firmly I clear away every question cluttering my brain except the one I most want an answer to. Should I sell the house or keep my share and partner with Cameron?

Poppy finishes her tea first. She stops drinking when there is a tablespoon of tea left in her cup. She already knows what to do. She swirls it three times and then turns over the cup and claps it gently onto the waiting saucer, upside down. She looks at me expectantly.

"I want to know if Freddie and I are making the right decision to buy the brewery," she confides, looking a little nervous.

"I thought it was a done deal," I tell her, surprised.

"It is," she says reluctantly, "But it's a big change, you know. To move and start a new business. I'd just like confirmation. Just to be sure."

"Okay, then let's see what the leaves say." I tap her cup three times gently on the bottom, then turn it over and hold it up to the light, studying the patterns in the bits of sodden tea leaf scattered around the inside of the cup. I have to think for a minute to recall the meaning of the symbols I see. I squint at the patterns, quieting my mind and filtering out any distractions.

"I see a wheel which symbolizes inevitable change or progress," I tell her. "And there's a fish which means..." I pause, trying to remember. "Good news is coming. And the last one looks like an arrow pointing up which means you're going in a good direction." I set the cup down and glance at Poppy. "It all looks positive, Pops."

She claps her hands, relieved and excited. "Oh good. I just got a little nervous, you know?"

"Louise?" I pick up her cup next. "Do you know the question you want an answer to?"

Louise nods. "I ken," she says.

"Okay, let's see what the leaves say," I take her almost empty cup and turn it over on its saucer, then tap it gently and flip it right side up.

"Huh, this is an interesting one," I peer at the tea leaves intently. "It looks like... a heart which can symbolize love and home, and a couple of squares, two squares, which stand for comfort and peace. And a tree which is the symbol for happiness." I glance up at her to see her eyes locked on me with a hungry look, eager and wary all at once.

"Do those symbols mean anything to you?" I ask. "Does it answer your question?"

"Aye, it does." She nods quickly and lets out a little sigh of relief. It sounds like she's been holding it for a while. "Thank you." She takes the cup and examines the patterns with interest.

Now it's my turn. Hesitantly, I drink the tea down to the last tablespoon, then invert my cup in the saucer and tap it three times. I turn it right side up and study the leaves carefully.

"What do you see?" Poppy asks, leaning over my shoulder.

For a moment I close my eyes and imagine Aunt Ellen here

with me, standing at my shoulder in her woolly cardigan, pointing out the symbols with her index finger. I open my eyes and see the patterns clearly, as though they're standing out in relief from the rest of the leaf detritus in the cup.

"An umbrella which represents difficulty." I murmur with a frown. That's an inauspicious start. "And a hammer which represents challenges overcome." I stare into the cup intently. "and a sun which represents energy, success, and new beginnings." I pause, mulling these over. "There's one more, a little house. If I remember right, that's the symbol for success in business."

Huh, this is interesting. What a portentous little cup of tea, packed with symbols and yet it clarifies nothing. Then I see it, one more symbol tucked up near the rim, the unmistakable outline of a heart. The universal symbol of love. Just like the symbol in Louise's cup. I set the teacup back in the saucer and frown, thinking of the possible meanings of all of these. Especially the heart.

"So what does it mean? Are you going to keep the house?" Poppy asks. She and Louise are looking at me expectantly. "All the symbols point to good things ahead, right?"

"Yes," I agree hesitantly, "it all sounds good but it doesn't clarify what I'll be successful doing," I point to the symbols in the cup. "You could just as easily interpret these to mean that I should sell the house. It's not clear." But I sneak another glance at the heart symbol, wondering how it fits into everything.

"If it's not clear, then let's not sell the house yet," Poppy urges. "Give Cam a chance to prove his concept. We can always sell if it doesn't work out, right?"

I hesitate, disappointed by the murky reading. I had allowed myself to hope that the tea leaves would guide me, but unfortunately they have not made things less confusing.

"Remember, the leaves rarely make the future clear on their own, hen," I hear Aunt Ellen's soft brogue in my ear in gentle admonishment. "The symbols offer people an invitation to pursue what they already know in their hearts is the right path to take."

Reading tea leaves, Aunt Ellen had always explained, was just a little bit of magic and a lot of intuition and insight into the human heart.

I touch the handle of the cup. Which is the right path to take? I ask myself. I honestly don't know. My heart wants to throw caution to the wind and say yes to Louise's request, but my head warns that I should choose another, less risky path. I glance up and Louise is staring at me wordlessly. I can see all the raw longing there, the hope and fear.

"Louise, why should I give your dad a chance?" I ask. "Why is he worth the risk?"

She thinks for a moment then says hesitantly, "Two years ago, when my mum..." She presses her lips together. She can't say the words, but I understand. When her mom overdosed.

"I was put in a foster home," she continues, her voice soft and a little nervous. "I was pretty sure that I was going to be stuck there until I aged out, like so many of the other older kids. I dinna think anyone would want to adopt me. No one really wants to take on a bairn my age. I ken I had a dad somewhere far away, but my mom had never told me anything much about him other than his name. I told the social worker what I ken of him, which wasna much at all. But then a few days later, Dad came for me." She swallows hard and darts a quick glance at me. "He dinnae ken I even existed before my mom died, but when they told him about me, he gave up everything, his whole life, and he came to get me."

She looks down at her hands, fidgeting with a silver ring on her thumb. "The first time I saw him, I was dead scared." She shrugs uncomfortably. "I mean, he was a total stranger. But he sat down next to me and looked me in the eye, and he made me a promise. He told me that it was him and me now, and that I dinnae ever have to worry because he wasna going anywhere ever. He promised me we'd make a home together, a real home where I dinnae have to move all the time. He told me..." She stops and swallows hard. "He told me he'd give his life for me, that I was his responsibility now. He told me he'd never leave me." She glances up, looking between Poppy and me, shooting us a wry smile. "I dinnae trust him right away, ye ken? I tested him hard for a while. But he kept his word. He has always kept his word." She frowns. "And so I think more than anyone, he deserves a chance to try to make his dream come true."

I'm touched by Louise's words and by the picture she paints of Cameron. What a good man he is. What a noble goal he has, trying to make a good life for his daughter. With uncanny intuition, Poppy senses me weakening and begins to press her advantage.

"If you say yes, you can negotiate free cheese from Cam every weekend for the rest of your life," she tells me in a stage whisper.

I roll my eyes at her blatant attempt to sway me. Free cheese for life sounds like a dream come true. Still... I think of my little cottage on Bainbridge Island. Do I really want to wait to make that dream come true and risk possible financial loss if Cameron cannot make his business idea profitable? I hate risk...

But then I make the mistake of glancing at Louise. I think of Cameron dropping everything to come for her, promising her he would care for her and make a home for her. He's worked tirelessly to try to make that happen. If I sell the house from under them, they'll have to start all over somewhere else. I have no doubt Cameron can build a stable home and provide for Louise anywhere. He's reliable and resourceful. But it would be costly for them to start all over. And if they did go somewhere else, I would not get to be a part of whatever they built, even if I'm planning on being a silent partner from a distance. At least I would still be a part of it in a way.

"Okay," I say, making a snap choice. I am going to follow my heart and see where it takes me. The tea leaves all point to success in business and new beginnings. I have a feeling this is the right way. "I'll give Cameron a chance to see if this business idea of his can succeed."

"For real?" Louise exclaims, beaming at me, her eyes lit up like stars.

"Yes!" Poppy shrieks happily and pumps her fist in the air in victory.

At that exact moment, the kitchen door flies open with a bang. We all shriek as a tall, looming figure ducks through the doorway. It's Cam, coppery hair hanging loose, breathing hard. He's not wearing a kilt, but a t-shirt and pair of dark green joggers that look better than they should on him. The dogs lift their heads and woof an alarm, then realize who it is and go back to sleep immediately.

"Louise," Cameron stops to catch his breath. "What are you thinking? Dinnae leave like that again, lass, aye? My mind was spinning like a wee top, imagining all sorts of terrible things when I saw your bedroom window open and you nowhere to be seen."

"You snuck out your window?" I ask in surprise.

Louise hangs her head and nods. "I'm sorry, Dad," she says in a small voice. Cameron rounds the island and places a hand on her shoulder, bending down to her level.

"I'm not mad at you, lass," he says gently. "Just worried for you. It's my job as your dad, okay?"

She nods.

"Well don't be too mad. Your daughter just saved your dream job," I tell him.

"She did what?" Cameron looks up, confused.

"She came to try to convince me not to sell the house," I tell him. "And she succeeded. I'll give you a year as your silent partner to see if you can turn a profit."

"Really?" A huge grin spread across Cameron's face, sweet and slow as treacle. Then he gives a Scottish war whoop that could raise centuries of his dead clansmen and in one smooth motion picks me up off the ground and crushes me to his chest, pressing a resounding kiss on the top of my head. I squeak in surprise.

"Thank you," he whispers in my ear, his voice breaking on the words. Over his shoulder I see Poppy's eyebrow wing upward in astonishment. She eats a shortbread finger as though she's watching a very riveting movie. I bury my nose in the shoulder of Cameron's old worn tee shirt and try to smell him without being obvious. He smells like warm sleep and baking things, and that hint of good peaty whisky and woodsmoke. Absolutely delicious. I don't want him to ever put me down.

"We have to hash out the terms," I tell him firmly.

"Aye, of course," he agrees. Slowly he sets me back on my feet. We're standing very close together.

"Here's what I'm offering," I tell him. "Poppy will sell her half share of the house to you. I'll keep my half share and be a silent partner in your business. I'll give you a year to prove you can start turning a profit. If by the end of a year, you still can't make the restaurant idea profitable, I want out. You can buy me out of my half of the house, or if you cannot afford to do that, we sell the house entirely." I look at him firmly, waiting to see what he says.

He considers the offer and nods. "Okay. I accept the terms." He sticks out his hand and we shake on it. I let go reluctantly.

I don't quite know why I've made the choice I have. Maybe sympathy or empathy or curiosity? Whatever the reason, I'm not sorry. It's still risky, but somehow the risk feels worth it. I still have the tidy nest egg tucked away for my down payment on my cottage. Either way, I will get my cottage on Bainbridge Island. It's just a matter of timing.

If Cameron's business does not succeed, we will sell the house in a year and I will buy my cottage sooner rather than later. And if Cameron's business does succeed... then I'll stay in my condo and keep consulting for a few more years and save up more money until I can afford to buy the cottage without the proceeds from the sale of the manor house.

Either way, I want to give Cameron a chance to make good on his promise to Louise. I want to see if his business idea can actually succeed. If that means I might have to continue at my job for longer than I'd planned, I'm willing to do that if it gives Cameron and Louise the chance to make a go of it. It's worth it to me.

I think of what we will need to do to make this official. I'll have to tell the Butlers we are not selling the house, and Cameron and I will need to be thorough, with contracts and attorneys to protect all parties involved.

I glance up and find Cameron gazing down at me. Our eyes catch and hold, and I see gratitude and appreciation and relief in those olive-green depths.

"Thank you, Avery," he says softly, and it feels like a caress. I think of our incendiary kiss right here in this kitchen last night. Somehow this stubborn, red headed giant of a man has lit a long dormant spark in my heart. I'm willing to take a risk for him. That feels big to me.

"You're welcome." I smile back at him, happy that I can give him the chance he deserves.

I think of the symbols in the tea leaves – success in business, new beginnings, and that pesky little heart. What does it all mean? Whatever it is, I have a good feeling about whatever the future holds. After standing so long in the shadows of guilt and grief, I am finally stepping into a future filled with bright possibility. What could possibly stop me?

Chapter 18

"**A**very, Avery!"

I half stir at the insistent pounding on my bedroom door. Unable to sleep again after the late-night excitement of the tea leaves and my decision, I took another Ambien before bed and am in the midst of a weird, drugged dream where I'm toasting marshmallows around a campfire with Cameron. I swear I can smell the woodsmoke. It feels so real.

The door to my room crashes open and I come awake to find Cameron looming over my bed, his worried face peering into mine. It's just turning light outside, the sky grey through the window.

"Whaa?" I blink sleepily in confusion.

"The kitchen is on fire," Cameron tells me matter of factly. "We must get out."

"WHAT?" I sit up, looking around wildly. The campfire smell was not just a dream. My bedroom is a little hazy with smoke. I cough and my eyes start watering.

"Come on. Everyone else is outside," Cameron grabs my

arm, his voice rough and urgent. "We dinna have a moment to spare. The fire's spreading."

"I need my computer and purse," Panicked, I scramble from the bed and try to stand up but immediately feel light-headed and sit back down again. It's the Ambien. I can't think straight.

"There's no time, lass." With a low Scottish oath of exasperation, Cameron scoops me up in his arms, cradles me to his chest, and strides from the bedroom at a pace that is just shy of a run. I glance back longingly at my purse and computer, then wrap my arms around his neck and hang on tight as I bounce down the grand staircase in Cameron's arms, feeling dizzy and disoriented from the smoke and the Ambien still in my bloodstream. I can hear a loud crackling and popping sound and the distant wail of a fire engine.

Outside Cameron sets me hastily on the front lawn next to Poppy who is clutching the children and watching flames shoot from the windows of the kitchen. Her expression is stricken and she's struggling not to cry. Grant is sobbing, his face buried against her hip. Maeve holds Poppy's hand, silent tears streaming down her face. Freddie is restraining the dogs who are going crazy. He's got them by the collars and is shouting at them to quiet down. We are all barefoot and shivering in the chilly dawn. A very light rain is misting down around us.

"What happened?" I ask Poppy, watching in horror.

She is staring wide eyed at the fire which seems to be growing. I can see flames licking from the windows up the exterior walls to the roof. "Where are the firefighters?" she shrugs helplessly, looking lost. "The dogs woke us up barking," she says. "Cam came a moment later and pounded on our door. He was just coming up to the house to get an early start this morning and he saw smoke pouring from the kitchen windows. By the time he got to the house and opened the door to the kitchen, the fire was too big. He called the fire department while Freddie got us and the dogs out." She looks at me, eyes wide and worried. "If Cam hadn't come, if the dogs hadn't alerted us..."

She clutches both the twins closer to her. Maeve is gripping her hand, watching the fire in horror. Grant wails even louder. He keeps peeking at the flames and then burying his face against Poppy's leg. We stand barefoot and shivering, watching helplessly as the flames grow. There is absolutely nothing we can do but wait. The sound of the fire engine siren grows louder and a moment later the fire service peels down the drive. Within minutes the place is swarming with fire personnel unrolling hoses and shouting orders.

"Dad?" It's Louise, running up the lane from their cottage, still in her pajamas. "What's happening? I heard the fire trucks." She stops short when she sees the flames. "Oh no." Her face crumples.

Cameron comes over and puts his arm around her. "Dinnae worry, wean. It will be okay," he says soothingly. "They'll get control of it in no time."

"What about your book of ideas?" she asks anxiously. "Did you get it?"

He shakes his head. "Dinnae have time," he says shortly. "I'd more important things to save." He glances in my direction, and I realize he means me. He chose me over the binder of ideas he described as the most valuable thing he owns. I press my hand to my chest, moved by the sacrifice.

Poppy puts her arm around Louise's shoulders and together we stand and watch the commotion. Freddie hauls the dogs to the stables to safely contain them until everything calms down. Cameron goes to see if he can lend a hand to the fire service. We watch the activity for several minutes in silence. It appears they're getting the blaze under control fairly quickly.

"I'm so sorry, Aves," Poppy looks at me guiltily. "With the dogs and the kids and the chaos, we didn't realize you weren't with us at first. Freddie pounded on your door when we were getting the kids out of the house. We were all out here on the lawn before we realized you were still inside." She meets my gaze and says softly, "When he realized you were still inside, Cam didn't hesitate. He went right for you. Freddie offered to go, but Cam just ran back in without a word." She holds my gaze for a moment, then turns back to watch the fire crew. They seem to have put out the fire, though smoke is still billowing in acrid waves from the kitchen. It will be a nightmare of a clean-up process, and who knows just how much damage has been done, but the rest of the house looks sound. I think the fire was contained to the kitchen, thankfully. I don't quite know what to think about what she told me about Cameron. He let his most precious possession go without hesitation to come save me.

A few minutes later, Cameron and Freddie return with a firefighter dressed in a khaki uniform with reflective stripes and a neon yellow helmet. In the grey of early morning, Cameron looks tired and drawn. He runs a hand over his face and his fingers leave sooty streaks. The air smells like a bonfire mixed with a harsh chemical odor and the underlying damp brine of the sea.

"Well folks, you're lucky you caught the fire so early," the woman tells us somberly. "We were able to contain the fire to just the kitchen. The damage is extensive, but localized. It looks like, from our initial assessment, faulty wiring on this is to blame?" She holds up the mangled, melted remains of the ancient toaster.

Poppy groans and puts her head in her hands. "I knew we should have replaced that years ago," she laments. Freddie moves to comfort her.

Grant peeks out from under Poppy's arm. "Now the fire is all gone, I'm hungry," he announces. "Mummy, can I have toast and jam?"

Freddie ruffles Grant's hair. "No toast this morning, I'm afraid, ya wee rascal." He looks pained as his eyes go to the toaster.

Cameron moves a few feet away and speaks at length to the firefighter. After a few minutes he comes back to us. "The fire service has it in hand now. They're going to finish up here. Why don't we all go down to the cottage, and I'll make us some breakfast. Then we can figure out what to do next."

Silently, we follow him down the footpath to the caretaker's cottage. It's been years since I set foot in the small stone house. The lower level is mostly an open concept living room/dining area which Cameron has made snug and homey with a squashy plaid couch, a coffee table littered with books, a basket of woolen blankets, and a wood stove that is warming the place nicely. A small galley kitchen completes the main level. Up the narrow stairs I know there is a bathroom sandwiched between two small gabled bedrooms with views of the sea.

Freddie retrieved the dogs from the stable and they both settle down by the stove, vigilant but quiet. Louise pulls out a board game, Sorry this time, and the twins start to play with her. Cameron heats water for tea and I make everyone a cuppa while he whips up breakfast in the kitchen. Freddie and Poppy are sitting at one end of the table, heads together, murmuring quietly, so I take my tea into the kitchen and offer to help. Cameron hands me a bowl and a dozen eggs and asks me to crack and scramble them. He's frying square slices of Lorne sausage in a skillet.

"Is the damage a lot, do you think?" I ask quietly.

"Aye, bad enough," he says grimly. "I'm guessing we're looking at an entirely new kitchen at minimum." He closes his eyes and shakes his head, muttering a few choice words in Gaelic.

"We were so close," he says with resignation. "This changes everything."

I crack eggs into the bowl, mind spinning. He's right. This does change everything. It essentially shuts down Cameron's operation for as long as it takes to repair the kitchen. From the look of the size of the fire in that room, it's going to be a big and costly repair. And probably take awhile. Where will the money come from? How long will it take? I know we have insurance on the house, but there will be a sizable deductible. Who will pay for that? This affects all of us and puts all of our plans in jeopardy. This is a disaster from all angles.

I whip the eggs and try not to borrow trouble, but my mind goes back to last night, to the symbols I saw in my teacup. An umbrella, representing difficulty. How prescient. I had no idea how quickly that difficulty would come upon us.

After a somber breakfast, we make a unanimous decision that the children will skip school today under the circumstances. The kids go back to their game of Sorry, and Cameron brews another pot of tea. Then we strategize.

"You can eat with Louise and me down here until the kitchen is working again," Cameron offers.

"And we can set up a hot plate and a new toaster and microwave in the dining room," Freddie adds. "And maybe one of those small refrigerators for the essentials."

"A curse on that old toaster!" Poppy fumes. "Why were we so cheap and didn't get a new one?"

"What's done is done, love," Freddie says gently, placing his hand on Poppy's and giving it a squeeze. "No use regretting what we canna change. We're planning to move in two months anyway, so let's keep that in mind. Plus we've got the insurance. They'll cover the damages."

Poppy makes a little moan. "But we raised the deductible

last year," she reminds him. "Because we were trying to cut costs. We'll have to cover twenty percent of the damages."

"Aye," Freddie nods, looking dismayed. "I'd forgotten that bit. Bugger all, but that will be expensive. And we can't finalize buying the brewery until we sell to Cam but now..." He looks uncertainly at his brother.

"I'm scuppered," Cameron announces calmly. He tips a splash of whisky into his tea and offers some to Freddie who accepts. "Losing the kitchen will put me back many months on the permits to open properly as well as the time and money I'll lose without a functional kitchen." He looks around the table and raises his glass in resignation. "We were barely scraping by as is, trying to keep going until the permits went through to let us open properly. Now there's no way I can hold out another four or six months. And I dinnae think you can sell the house or I can buy the house without a functional kitchen. No bank will allow a mortgage on a house with no working kitchen. So now that plan is sunk." He takes a swig of tea with a stoic resignation.

I consider the dilemma. Everyone's plan is sunk, actually. No one can get a mortgage on a property with no working kitchen, which means Cameron cannot buy out Poppy and Freddie, they can't buy their brewery, and even if we decided to sell the house as-is, no buyer would be able to get a mortgage. Any way you slice it, we're all stuck. Until I remember the Butlers. I texted Amir before I went to bed last night and let him know we would not be selling the house. But now...

"Maybe there's still a way out," I say slowly. "The Butlers wanted the house, but they're not going to start using it until Christmas at least. They were making an all-cash offer, so they don't need a mortgage. Maybe they'd still want to buy it, for a lower price of course. They'd have time to finish kitchen renovations before Christmas." It doesn't solve Cameron's problem, but it solves the issue for Poppy and Freddie, and for me. I take my phone out. "Should I text Amir and see if they're still interested, even with the fire damage?"

Freddie looks at Cameron and then at Poppy. "Why not?" he asks with a shrug. "Wouldn't hurt to know our options at this point."

I send the text and sip my tea. Somehow pushing that button feels like admitting defeat. But what else can we do? Cameron is staring into the distance, his face drawn. I've never known him to be cowed by anything, but he looks now like a man staring at his own execution.

"We came so close to making it all work," Poppy sighs sadly and rests her head on her hand. We're all exhausted and smokey and shaken. There's a rap on the door and when Cameron rises to answer it, the same khaki clad firefighter is standing there. They talk for a moment, and he turns back to us.

"The fire services are finished," he says. "It's safe to go back in the house. We need to stay out of the kitchen until the insurance agent can come assess the damage, but the rest of the house is undamaged."

"Everything is going to smell like a bonfire," Poppy exclaims in chagrin. "Even me." She sniffs her pajamas and wrinkles her nose.

"I'd better go call the insurance company and start filing a claim," Freddie says with a sigh.

"Ugh, and how are we going to pay for the repairs?" Poppy wails. Freddie claps her on the shoulder.

"It'll be okay," he says, but I can tell he's worried.

I check my phone and pray for a miracle.

* * *

Clients still want the house. Expect new offer with reduced price today. The text from Amir comes partway through the afternoon while I'm hanging out with the twins building Legos in the least smokey room of the house while Poppy and Freddie meet with an insurance adjuster. They've spent the day handling the practicalities of the fire. After the adjuster leaves, Freddie takes the kids into town with him to run an errand, and I slip down to the dining room to grab a cup of tea and a handful of tea biscuits, then head outside. It's turned into a lovely day, though the smell of soot and ashes still lingers around the house. I sit on the front lawn and sip my tea.

"This view never gets old, does it?" Poppy sighs, coming up next to me. She's wearing her black rain wellies and her clothes are damp and streaked with soot. She sits down and helps herself to one of the Jammie Dodgers I brought out. I tell her about Amir's text.

"You think we should take the offer, then?" she asks tiredly.

I bite into a Jaffa Cake. "What choice do we have? It's the only way I see this working out. You still get your half of the sale price to pay for the brewery. I can buy my cottage on the bay, and we all get on with our lives."

"What about Cam and Louise?" Poppy asks.

I hesitate. "They find somewhere else. Cameron will land on his feet."

Even as I say it, I know the likelihood of him finding another property that works for his idea is very slim. He can only afford half the cost of this house, and it has everything he needs to run his business. Where else will he find a property he can afford that has land, a barn, gardens, rooms and space for a restaurant, café and small store? Anything else like this will be far more than he can afford.

"I guess they'll move into town. I know of at least two restaurants that will hire him as head chef in a heartbeat," Poppy says wistfully. "I just wish we could have made it work." She helps herself to a digestive biscuit. "You sure there's not another way?" She eyes me speculatively.

I take a sip of tea and shake my head. "You heard Cameron," I tell her. "Even if we could scrape together the money for the kitchen repairs, he can't afford to wait for the renovation to be done before he gets his business up and running. I don't see how this can work. Before the fire, yes, but now?"

"I just don't want to give up yet," Poppy says, setting her chin with a familiar stubborn gesture. "I bet there's a way if we try hard enough."

"It's too risky now, Pops." I shake my head. "I was willing to assume some risk before the fire, but now... it feels like too much uncertainty, too great a risk. There are too many moving parts." I pop the rest of my Jaffa Cake in my mouth. I don't even taste it. My stomach feels like lead.

Poppy turns to me and gives me a hard stare. "I've never taken you for a coward," she says briskly. "But now I see I was wrong."

"What's that supposed to mean?" I ask indignantly.

She shakes her head. "Can't you see how good this is? You love all of this - me and Freddie and the twins, this house and Oban. You and Cameron are so good together, even if you're scared to admit it. I saw you the night of the garden party. You were glowing, and it wasn't just because Cam is the hottest chef in the West Highlands. It's because you got to be part of something, part of a family, part of building something together. You love all of this, so why are you not willing to fight for it?"

I gape at her. Where did this sudden burst of candor come from? My carefree sister isn't pulling any punches.

"I was willing to fight for it," I protest. "I said yes to Cameron. I was giving it a go."

"But now you're done?" Poppy snorts. "As soon as things get hard you bail? You're so afraid to risk, so afraid you might fail again, that you're willing to give up all this potential for goodness in your life at the first sign of difficulty. If you're not careful, Avery, you're going to end up alone wearing a blanket with sleeves, eating way more cheese than is good for one person and reading romance novels set in Scotland but never actually living a romance story of your own."

Ouch! "How do you know about the romance novels?" I demand.

Poppy looks shifty.

"You peeked in my suitcase?" I gape at her, indignant.

"It was an accident," She waves the accusation away. "I was trying to find that cardigan sweater you have that I like. I wanted to borrow it. But I found your book stash instead. Come on, Avery. Admit it. Your life is sad."

I roll my eyes. "Okay yes, it's a little sad. But I like it this way. It's tidy."

Poppy turns to me, her expression indignant. "Are you seriously going to tell me that you're going to turn down the possibility of being close to family, saving our ancestral home, doing something new and exciting, and maybe even having a real romance with a super hot, super good guy so you can keep your life tidy?"

She says the word tidy like it's a swear word.

She wrinkles her nose at me, waiting.

I squirm. When she puts it like that...

"You make me sound pathetic!" I object.

Poppy's face softens. "Avery, I love you more than you can imagine, so don't take this the wrong way, but if you take the easy way out and deny yourself every good thing so you can stay alone and not have to risk, I will never forgive you." She grabs my last biscuit, a bourbon cream, and stuffs it in her mouth. "Oh, and by the way, don't think I didn't notice that all those novels feature men who look suspiciously exactly like Cam!" she says around the crumbs. Then she gets to her feet and leaves me staring after her, filled with indignation and the sneaking suspicion that she may just be right about everything.

Chapter 19

"I can't believe I'm doing this," I mutter as I shift gears and navigate the Mini through the tight turns of the lane leading to town. Next to me in my bag, Aunt Ellen's favorite teacup is rattling in its saucer. I don't know what possessed me to bring it from Chicago, but I did. Now I have such a strong feeling I need to set foot somewhere I never thought I'd go again and take this teacup with me.

Once in downtown Oban, I park and walk the few blocks north, quickly passing Gelatoburger and Spice World. I'm carrying the teacup gently in my bag under my arm. It clinks as I walk. At the craft store I pause. Fiona is inside on a ladder, wrestling skeins of yarn onto a top shelf. I knock gently on the window and she comes down immediately and opens the door, throwing her arms around me.

"I heard about the fire!" she says, pulling back, her eyes worried. Of course she did. In a small town, news travels fast.

"We're all fine. Just the kitchen got damaged," I reassure her. "And it was overdue for a renovation anyway. It'll be okay."

"I'll bring you all a pot of stew this week," she says, "since you don't have a working kitchen. When things calm down maybe we can have a cuppa and a good long catch up?"

"I'd love that," I tell her. "Really. But right now I've got to run. There's something I have to do."

Leaving the craft shop, I head north, passing the tartan shops and Hinba. For a moment I'm tempted to pop in for a coffee and forget the reason I've come to town, but I force myself to walk past, intent on a destination I haven't set foot in for a decade. I don't know why, but I know I must come here. It feels important.

The door looks the same. White and paneled with six panes of glass. The storefront is on a corner with huge windows so the daylight floods in even on the greyest winter mornings. I force myself to open the door and step inside. At first glance, I am disoriented. Everything is different. No wall of old fashioned shelved with glass jars of loose leaf tea from around the world. And the smell of jasmine, heather, and slightly bitter tea leaves has been replaced by the sunshiny warm aroma of good whisky. I don't know what I was expecting, but there are no ghostly presences here. I'm surprised to discover that even the memory of my failure doesn't sting quite so badly in this familiar space

"Good afternoon. May I help you?" A young man in a very new looking kilt asks me politely.

I stare at him a moment, startled that he is not Aunt Ellen. He blinks at my silence.

"Sorry, just browsing." I tell him, and he nods.

"I'll be in the back then. Take your time and let me know if you need anything.

I murmur thanks and he disappears into the back. I'm alone in the shop. Relieved, I take a long, slow breath, trying to reconcile all my years of memories with the present. Everything is different now. And yet here I am, back again, seeking direction in this place that once meant so much to Aunt Ellen and to me.

"I need help, Aunt Ellen," I say softly to the empty shop. "Can you help me?" I blow out a breath I've been holding. I'm back here at last, seeking clarity. What I have not admitted to anyone, not even to myself until now, is that accepting the Butlers offer to buy the house is not our only option. There is a far riskier one. I have a good chunk of money squirreled away for a down payment for my cottage on the bay. I could use my down payment to pay for the deductible for the kitchen repair project. The insurance would cover the rest. Poppy and Freddie could still buy the brewery and move to Fort William. Cameron could still buy out their half of the house. He'd have some lean months before the kitchen was complete, but perhaps he could still manage to offer some things from his own kitchen? Catered picnics in scenic spots around Oban? Events where he cooks on site? Cameron had mentioned short term renters, but I think we could let out some of the guest rooms to longer term renters instead. The cost of living is high in Oban. There are sure to be a few wait staff or shop employees who would appreciate renting a good room in a gracious local manor house. That would help cover costs until we could get the restaurant up and running.

The fact is that if I wanted to, I could still make it possible for Cameron and Louise to stay and for Cameron to open his restaurant. But it feels risky to have so much sunk cost in this place I've been trying to escape for so long. If the business failed, I would get my money back in a year when we sold the house, but if the business is successful... there is the rub. All my money would be invested in this house and business. There would be no cottage on the bay. I would be trading my dream and keeping Haye House instead. Is it worth the trade? It scares me to think of it.

"I don't know what to do," I murmur. For a moment I picture it. Me at Haye House, side by side with Cameron as an active business partner. I could move back to Scotland, to Haye House, and help Cameron build a business that flourishes. We could use the time during the renovations to build a marketing strategy. I've learned a huge amount about what not to do from watching so many businesses crash and burn over the years. Now I could put all that knowledge to good use and help ensure the success of Cameron's venture. I have little interest in being hands-on in the garden or kitchen, except maybe to make more cheese, but the thought of using all I've gleaned from my jobs over the years to actually help something succeed is exciting.

I'm a woman of spreadsheets and calculators, and that won't change, but what if I could use my strengths to help a business grow and thrive, not just end as smoothly as possible? And what if I did that from my family home, with Cameron? The thought is thrilling and terrifying. I want it so much it almost paralyzes me. Do I dare risk it? There are so many reasons to say no. It could go terribly wrong in a dozen different ways. I would have to endure the risk of failure again, and the possibility of heart-break too.

I think of the designs in my teacup from last night. It feels like a century ago already. An umbrella which represents difficulty. Boy did that one come true fast. And a hammer which represents overcoming challenges, and a sun which represents energy, success and new beginnings. A little house, the symbol of success in business. And the final one, a heart, the universal symbol of love.

"Where are the symbols pointing?" I whisper aloud, "What is the right path?" I can feel Aunt Ellen's presence here.

I pull out the teacup and a thermos of loose leaf tea. I pour the tea leaves into the cup and glance around furtively. No one is nearby. Then I swirl the leaves in the cup three times, drink the tea, and turn the cup over on the saucer.

"Show me what to do," I plead. I pick up the cup and study

the patterns of the tea leaves. Lines for change. A rabbit to symbolize courage needed to overcome adversity. And there it is again, up in the corner away from the other symbols. A heart. Love.

"What do these symbols mean?" I whisper. "What should I do?"

"Always tell them what you see," I hear the echo of Aunt Ellen's Scottish burr like she's standing at my shoulder. "Tell the truth and nothing more, then leave it be," she continues. "They'll accept the invitation the tea leaves offer or they won't." She shrugs her slightly stooped, boney shoulders in her home-made wool cardigan. "All we can do is offer the invitation. It's up to them to decide what they do with it."

I understand what she is saying. She will not tell me what to do. No one can. I look at the symbols once more. I search my own heart. And there I find the answer.

"Okay," I whisper back to her. "I know what I have to do."

There is no response, but in the silence I swear I can feel her smile.

When I return to the house an hour later, I don't head all the way to the big manor house. Instead I follow a twisty little drive off to the side until I reach the caretaker's cottage. It's suppertime and everyone is crammed inside eating smoked ham soup and Cameron's fresh bread. A chorus of greetings rises from the table when I step into the room. Duffy and Daisy woof and wag their tails, crowding around. Cameron gets up and ladles a bowl for me, gesturing for me to sit. I don't. Instead I hand him a bottle of wine I bought at the shop that used to be The Thistle Tea Room. I felt I had to when the shopkeeper came out suddenly and found me standing there looking at a teacup.

"The soup smells delicious," I tell Cameron, "But first I have something to say."

The babble of conversation dies down and every eye is on me. I go to Poppy and place a single piece of A4 paper beside her place.

"What's this?" she asks, mouth full of bread.

"It's a receipt for a bank transfer from my bank account to yours for the amount of fifty thousand pounds. I hope that will be enough to cover the deductible amount for the kitchen repairs."

Flustered, Poppy chokes and has to grab her glass of water. "What does this mean?" she asks in confusion when she's regained her breath. I glance up and see Cameron's eyes on me with a look so intent he could probably bore a hole through glass.

"It means I'm all in."

No one says anything.

"I told the Butlers we're not selling the house," I clarify. "We'll renovate the kitchen and Cameron can start his business as planned when it's done."

At my words, Freddie whoops in a highly uncharacteristic display of emotion. Poppy gasps and jumps up, grabbing me in a tight hug.

"I'm so proud of you!" she whispers fiercely.

When she lets me go, Cameron is waiting for me. He wraps his arms around me. "Thank you," he whispers against my hair. I loop my arms around his neck and let myself nestle against him for just a moment. "You're welcome." I tell him. "I'm not just doing this for you. I'm doing it for all of us, especially me." I raise my head and my voice. "Louise convinced me," I say loud enough that she can hear. She looks up, startled, something bright and hopeful sparking to life in her gaze.

"Are you getting married?" Grant pipes up, eyeing our embrace with chagrin. Poppy shushes him, but Cameron and I break apart with a chuckle.

"We still have a lot of details to work through," I tell him. "I've made a spreadsheet."

"Of course you have," he says calmly. "But first have some soup."

As I sit and eat the delicious soup, I gaze around the table. We have so much we have to figure out, both financially and practically. It's going to take us months to get everything settled. Weirdly, this makes me feel energized, I realize happily. I like nothing more than a challenge, and this is the best kind, fighting for people and a place I love. I scrape my bowl clean, then pause to text Amir.

Call me crazy but we're going to keep the house. I hope the Butlers enjoy their chateau. Thanks for everything.

A moment later I get a reply text. **Good luck, darling** and a heart emoji. I tuck my phone away. I definitely owe him a nice sushi dinner next time I'm in L.A..

Then I realize I've forgotten something.

"One more thing." I reach into the shopping bag I carried in with me and pull out a brand new toaster. I set it on the table. Poppy groans.

"A very timely gift," Freddie says seriously. "How thoughtful."

Cameron comes out of the kitchen with glasses of whisky, one for each of the adults. He hands them around. "Slainte Mhath." Cameron raises his glass. "To new beginnings." His olive-green eyes meet mine, filled to the brim with things he has not yet had a chance to say. I feel the same, but there will be time. Now there is time for everything.

"And to electronics that won't catch fire," I reply.

We laugh and toast and drink.

Epilogue

One year later

"We did it!" I crow jubilantly, looking around in exhausted glee at the almost empty dining room. A few minutes ago it was packed with guests as we hosted our first dinner featuring a locally sourced seven course tasting menu and wine pairings. Now the last few guests are getting into their cars. The evening went perfectly.

"Avery, congratulations. Tell Cam that the meal was dead brilliant," Fiona comes up to me and gives me a huge hug. She's wearing a shapeless sort of knit wrap that makes her look a little like a mushroom. "Come by the shop next week and we can have a dram together." She blows an air kiss and heads out the front doors.

Since I decided to stay in Scotland, Fiona and I have rekindled our friendship. She is slightly better at handicrafts than she was a year ago, although her crafting skills are a work in progress as evidenced by the mushroom wrap tonight. I am thankful for her cheerful support this past year as we've labored long and hard to bring our joint vision to fruition.

As Fiona's car pulls out of the gravel drive, Cameron comes up and wraps his arms around me, kissing the top of my head fondly. He's wearing his kilt and chef's whites, and he smells deliciously of whisky and sugared fruit. I sniff him appreciatively, feeling exhausted and exhilarated at the same time. It's been a year of frustration, growth, toil, and triumph but finally we've arrived. It's Sunday night and Haye House Farm Collective has just finished the last event of its grand opening weekend.

We now sport a farm store open seven days a week where we sell Cameron's jams, chutneys and cheeses as well as a collection of local artisan-crafted products like bath soap made with foraged heather and kelp and even a few woolen goods from Fiona's store. Simple things she's managed to master like felted pot holders shaped like thistles. She's working on Highland cows and sheep felted wool Christmas ornaments, but we'll see how they turn out. We even sell the ubiquitous tartan scarves – though ours are locally and sustainably sourced – because it's Scotland and tourists love them.

We have a tea room open every day for lunch for high tea, and a dining room open every weekend for a set seven course tasting menu paired with local wines and spirits. The weekend dinners are booked out for four months already and the wait list is growing by the day. If my calculations are correct, and they usually are, we will be making a profit by next quarter.

"That was the best meal of my life," Poppy comes up to us and kisses Cameron's cheek and pulls me in for a tight hug. "Good job, both of you."

They've left the kids with Louise down at the cottage so they could enjoy our celebratory feast. Now they're the last guests to leave. Behind them our new busboy is clearing tables and in a minute, Cameron will head back to the kitchen to debrief the evening with Kenny and the small staff we've hired. Poppy and Freddie are beaming, enjoying a rare date night off. Despite the demands of their new business, they have discovered how much they enjoy brewing and being pub owners and the entire family is thriving in Fort William. I'm so happy for them.

"How's the shiny new kitchen?" Freddie asks, clapping Cameron on the back.

"A dream," Cameron replies.

I don't wish a house fire on anyone but the silver lining was a brand new, state of the art industrial kitchen that makes these dinners so much easier to pull off.

"This night calls for a toast," I announce. "The good stuff."

Cameron disappears and comes back with glasses and a bottle of Scotch. Freddie whistles when he sees the label. "A twenty-one-year-old limited release from the Oban Distillery? The good stuff indeed," he comments.

Cameron pours and hands each of us a glass. I look around as he does so, amazed by the changes a year has wrought. The house looks essentially the same, but it is buzzing with life and energy. He managed to mostly recreate his treasured binder of recipes and ideas with a little help from Dominic Warne who flew out from New Zealand for a week to advise us as we built the business. Over the past year, it's been wonderful to see Cameron's vision come to life. We've proven to be an excellent team. He handles the practical and creative aspects of the business and I handle the financial, marketing, and legal matters. It's been a joy to put my skills to use in this way. I'm also consulting part-time, using my metrics and spreadsheets and years of experience to help fledgling or struggling food-based businesses succeed. The income from consulting has helped keep Haye House Farm Collective afloat over this year of plans and renovations, and I enjoy these types of clients far more than I ever did before. I love helping to strengthen a good idea, not dismantle a bad one.

Cameron slips his arm around my waist and I rest my head on his shoulder. It still amazes me to think of what has happened between us personally as well. He's gone from least favorite human to... well... I raise my glass and the small diamond of my engagement ring catches the light. We've been engaged for two months now and are planning a small September wedding. I'll move from the big house down to the cottage after the wedding, and we'll settle into being a family of three. For now Louise and I are slowly building a relationship based on trust and friendship. I genuinely like her and I think she feels the same about me. She beats me every time at Sorry, but still neither of us can beat Maeve at Monopoly.

"To risks and rewards," Cameron says, raising his glass and giving me a knowing, sideways glance. He understands how much I risked, and how great the reward has been.

"Slainte Mhath." Freddie and Poppy murmur. We toast. The whisky slides down my throat smooth and warm and bright as though I'm swallowing a ray of sunshine. I look around, still feeling a touch of astonishment. How has it come to this, that I am back home in Scotland, with those I love, in the midst of a grand adventure I do not know the ending of?

"Aunt Ellen," I murmur, fondly scolding. "Did you arrange all of this?"

A delighted chuckle sounds low in my ear, and I swear I hear the faintest reply in her familiar brogue, "Ah hen, all I can do is offer the invitation. It's up to you to decide what you do with it." And then her voice again, softer this time. "*A h-uile là sona dhuibh 's gun là idir dona dhuibh.*"

I slowly translate the Gaelic in my head. *May all your days be happy ones.*

I raise my glass and take another sip, toasting the woman who helped make all this happen.

As I do, I have the sweetest premonition that Aunt Ellen's blessing is already coming true, and that our future will be filled with many happy days indeed.

THE END

Recipe for Scottish Cranachan

Cranachan (pronounced CRA-neh-kin) is a light, tasty traditional Scottish dessert. You can use this recipe as written or adjust any of the ingredient amounts to suit your individual taste. This recipe makes six portions. Enjoy!

Ingredients:

1/3 Cup oats (steel cut or regular)

1 ½ Cups fresh red raspberries

2 Cups heavy whipping cream

3 Tablespoons good whisky or Scotch

1 Tablespoon honey + more to drizzle on top

Instructions:

1. Heat a skillet over medium high heat. Add the oats and stir constantly until they are lightly toasted with a nutty aroma, about 3 to 4 minutes. Do not burn! Set aside.

2. Set aside ¼ cup raspberries for garnish. In a medium bowl, mash the remaining raspberries with a fork or place raspberries in a food processor and pulse lightly (just once or twice). You want a chunky raspberry puree, not a smooth one. Set aside.

3. In a large bowl, using a hand blender, whip the heavy cream and whisky together until stiff peaks form.

4. Fold the honey and the toasted oats into the whipped cream mixture.

5. Layer the dessert in a glass bowl (at least a 6 cup size) or in 6 serving glasses. Spoon a layer of raspberry puree into the bottom, then alternate with the cream mixture, and continue alternating layers. End with a whipped cream layer on the top.

6. Sprinkle with the fresh raspberries you set aside for garnish and drizzle with honey to taste.

Acknowledgments

A great big THANK YOU to the following wonderful folks who helped make this story better and brighter.

- Kylie Balstad, Ashley Hayes, and Matt LaCombe for their invaluable help in bringing this story to life and Kristin Bryant for the gorgeous cover design.
- Bestselling authors Marie Bostwick and Katherine Reay for being wonderfully smart and supportive book buddies. They are also delightful co-hosts of our weekly author interview show @The10minutebooktalk (check us out on Instagram, Facebook and YouTube).
- My generous and talented PNW author community. The delightful Bookstagram community united by their love of story.
- All my incredible independent bookstore friends around Puget Sound. A million thanks for supporting local authors. You are the best!
- Special thanks to the following ladies for reading this story early and offering keen insights: Jennifer Bester, Danielle Burk, Marie Bostwick, Cheryl Crawford, and Sarah Wolfe.
- Thanks to Sarah and Jared for venturing to Oban, Scotland with me for a research trip. So glad we didn't let car troubles and gale force winds deter us from having fun!

- For A and B, who bring such joy to my life. It's the greatest privilege to be your mom.
- And Y for joining me in Scotland for book research and being my adventure buddy and constant loving support for eighteen years!
- Lastly, for every reader who chooses to take a risk and grow. This story is from my heart to yours...

About the Author

Photo by Mallory MacDonald

Rachel Mae Linden is a novelist and international aid worker whose adventures in over fifty countries around the world provide excellent grist for her writing. She is the author of Recipe for a Charmed Life and The Magic of Lemon Drop Pie (now a Hallmark movie called The Magic of Lemon Drops) as well as several other novels. Currently Rachel lives with her family on a sweet little island in the Pacific Northwest where she enjoys creating stories about hope, courage and connection with a hint of romance and a touch of whimsy.

To connect with Rachel, visit her author website at www.rachellinden.com. There you can sign up for her newsletter and receive a special free gift in your inbox - a mini recipe book of Rachel's favorite recipes from her travels around the world! You can also connect with her on Instagram and Facebook.